SHADOW SQUADRON

BLACK ANCHOR

WRITTEN BY
CARL BOWEN

ILLUSTRATED BY
WILSON TORTOSA

COLORED BY
BENNY FUENTES

2012.241

AUTHORIZING

5514.108

Shadow Squadron is published by
Stone Arch Books,
A Capstone Imprint,
1710 Roe Crest Drive
North Mankato, MN 56003
www.capstoneyoungreaders.com

Cataloging-in-Publication Data is available on the Library of Congress website.

ISBN: 978-1-4965-2764-6

Printed in China.
042015 008902

CONTENTS

1316.981

2012.101

CLASSIFIED

SHADOW SQUADRON DOSSIER

CROSS, RYAN

RANK: Lieutenant Commander
BRANCH: Navy SEAL
PSYCH PROFILE: Cross is the team leader of Shadow Squadron. Control oriented and loyal, Cross insisted on hand-picking each member of his squad.

WALKER, ALONSO

RANK: Chief Petty Officer
BRANCH: Navy SEAL
PSYCH PROFILE: Walker is Shadow Squadron's second-in-command. His combat experience, skepticism, and distrustful nature make him a good counter-balance to Cross's leadership.

YAMASHITA, KIMIYO

RANK: Lieutenant
BRANCH: Army Ranger
PSYCH PROFILE: The team's sniper is an expert marksman and a true stoi[illegible] It seems his emotions are as stead[illegible] as his trigger finger.

SAND SPIDER

WRITTEN BY
CARL BOWEN

ILLUSTRATED BY
WILSON TORTOSA
AND
BENNY FUENTES

2012.241

CONTENTS

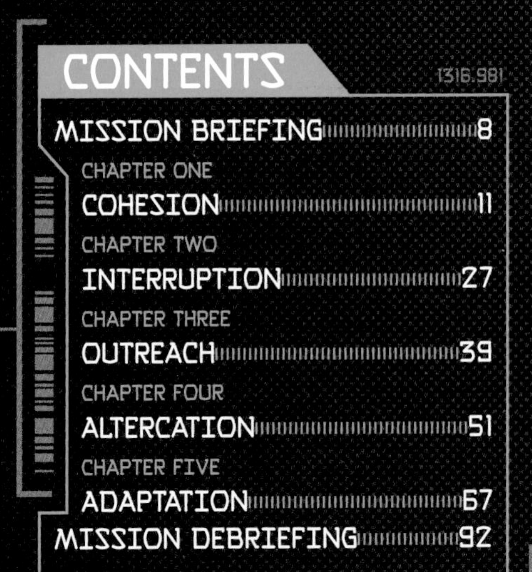

CLASSIFIED

SHADOW SQUADRON DOSSIER

CROSS, RYAN

RANK: Lieutenant Commander
BRANCH: Navy Seal
PSYCH PROFILE: Cross is the team leader of Shadow Squadron. Control oriented and loyal, Cross insisted on hand-picking each member of his squad.

WALKER, ALONSO

RANK: Chief Petty Officer
BRANCH: Navy Seal
PSYCH PROFILE: Walker is Shadow Squadron's second-in-command. His combat experience, skepticism, and distrustful nature make him a good counter-balance to Cross's leadership.

YAMASHITA, KIMIYO

RANK: Lieutenant
BRANCH: Army Ranger
PSYCH PROFILE: The team's sniper is an expert marksman and a true stoic. It seems his emotions are as steady as his trigger finger.

LANCASTER, MORGAN

RANK: Staff Sergeant
BRANCH: Air Force Combat Control
PSYCH PROFILE: The team's newest member is a tech expert who learns fast and has the ability to adapt to any combat situation.

JANNATI, ARAM

RANK: Second Lieutenant
BRANCH: Army Ranger
PSYCH PROFILE: Jannati serves as the team's linguist. His sharp eyes serve him well as a spotter, and he's usually paired with Yamashita on overwatch.

SHEPHERD, MARK

RANK: Lieutenant
BRANCH: Army (Green Beret)
PSYCH PROFILE: The heavy-weapons expert of the group, Shepherd's love of combat borders on unhealthy.

2019.681

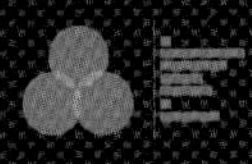

I've received an urgent call from a senator involved with Shadow Squadron's budget. To say he has a request is not entirely accurate -- it's more like a demand. In any event, if we want to keep receiving funding for the team, we have to head to Mali and rescue his kidnapped son.

I expect the team's cooperation to be top-notch after the extensive cohesion training we've undergone with our new combat controller, Morgan Lancaster.

– Lieutenant Commander Ryan Cross

3245.98

PRIMARY OBJECTIVE(S)

- Determine location of hostage
- Escort hostage to safety

SECONDARY OBJECTIVE(S)

- Avoid conflict with local forces

1932.789

0412.981

1624.054

5514.108

INTEL

DECRYPTING

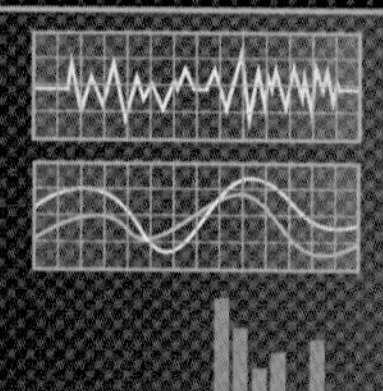

12345

COM CHATTER

- BRIEFING: information presented before a mission that is relevant to said mission
- COHESION: training required to help team members work together more effectively
- OPERATIVE: a secret agent or spy

3245.98

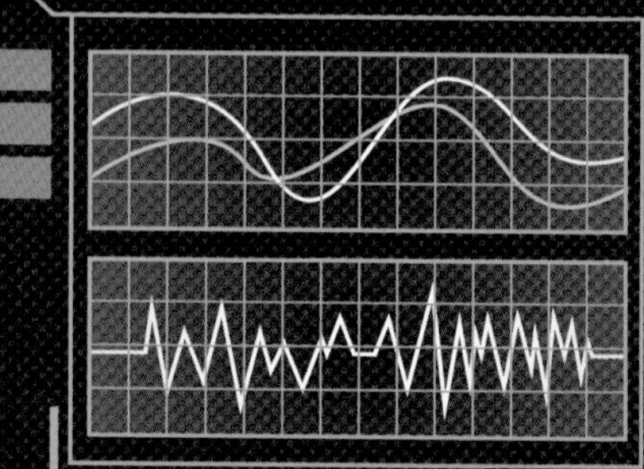

1324.014

CHAPTER ONE

COHESION

Lieutenant Commander Ryan Cross assembled his men in the briefing room as early as he dared, considering the previous evening's festivities. They'd held a going-away party for USAF Staff Sergeant Edgar Brighton, the team's former combat controller. The young soldier had been a member of the team since its creation, but he'd accepted a reassignment offer after a recent mission. From now on, he'd work for a highly classified psy-ops and cyber warfare division of the Department of Defense that promised to make better use of his intellect and technical skills.

That left Commander Cross with a hole to fill on his team. A rather big one, since Brighton was excellent at his job. But after a long period of paperwork evaluations and a handful of interviews, Cross was finally ready to introduce Brighton's replacement to the rest of the team.

That team was Shadow Squadron — a top-secret special missions unit. Assembled by the United States' Joint Special Operations Command, the unit was comprised of elite soldiers from all branches of the military. The team had soldiers from the Navy SEALs, Green Berets, Army Rangers, and the Marine Special Operations Regiment. They traveled all over the world rooting out terrorist threats, hunting international criminals, rescuing hostages, defending foreign leaders, and even fighting pirates. From one end of the world to the other, the team had showed up wherever the US government required military intervention but couldn't act openly for tactical, political, or legal reasons.

Cross's second-in-command was Chief Petty Officer Alonso Walker, a Navy SEAL like Cross. As usual, Walker arrived first, followed closely by the five remaining soldiers of Cross's team. Except for Sergeant Mark Shepherd, a Green Beret, none of them looked worse for the wear from their partying the night before. Shepherd was sporting a black eye from his ride on a mechanical bull at Brighton's going-away party. All of them sat quietly and glanced at the empty chair at the middle of the table. Brighton's absence was sorely felt.

"Let's get started," Cross said. He clicked on a computer touchpad built into the tabletop. The projector in the ceiling displayed the globe-and-crossed-swords emblem of Joint Special Operations Command on the computer whiteboard behind him. "With Staff Sergeant Brighton having moved on, we need to train his replacement and get the team back up to full cohesion."

The men nodded. When Shadow Squadron was created, the men had to go through nearly a year of special cohesion training. The purpose was to blend a group of individuals with different skills and military backgrounds into a functioning, singular unit. When Second Lieutenant Aram Jannati arrived from the Marines Special Operations Regiment to replace the

deceased Larssen, another month and a half of the same training was required to integrate him into the team. Now with the arrival of Brighton's replacement, another period of more cohesion training lay ahead of them.

Sergeant Shepherd spoke up first. "So who's the new guy? And when's he getting here?"

Cross grinned. "Now," he said. He tapped a button next to the touchpad on the table, keying an intercom. "Send Lancaster in," he said in the intercom microphone's direction.

"Sir," came the reply from a nearby speaker.

All the men turned in expectation as the door opened as the newest member of Shadow Squadron entered the room.

"Gentlemen," Cross said, "this is Staff Sergeant Morgan Lancaster, US Air Force Combat Controller."

"Morning," Sergeant Lancaster said. She closed the door behind her and waited. For what seemed like a long time, no one spoke or moved. Cross waited to see how his men would react to his choice.

As he'd privately hoped, it was Shepherd who broke the silence.

"A girl," Shepherd said. He stood up and crossed over to stand in front of her. The top of Lancaster's head came up even with Shepherd's Adam's apple, so when he stopped she had to look up at him. "I thought you'd be, um . . . prettier."

Anger flashed in Chief Walker's face. He leaned forward and opened his mouth to say something, but Cross stopped him with a glance and a subtle wave of his hand. Walker remained silent despite his obvious frustration.

"I beg your pardon?" Lancaster said to Shepherd.

"You know, like if you have to distract a guard with your pretty smile," Shepherd went on, as if what he was saying was completely reasonable. "Or if you have to infiltrate a high class society function in a fancy evening dress. You look way too tough to do any of that, if you ask me."

Lancaster let a hint of a smile play around the corner of her mouth. "Hello, Mark. It's good to see you haven't changed at all."

Shepherd dropped the act and broke out in a huge grin. He put out a hand and Lancaster shook it. "Hey, Morgan," he said. "It's been a long time. How's your sister doing?"

"Better off," Lancaster said. Her grin was bigger than Shepherd's now.

Walker relaxed a little. "So you two know each other," he said.

"Yeah, Chief," Shepherd said over his shoulder. "We went to high school together. I dated her sister." He turned back to Lancaster. "Still in the Air Force, huh? How mad are your folks about that?"

Lancaster shrugged. "They're mostly over it," she said. "Mostly, they just shake their heads in disappointment whenever someone asks if I joined the Navy like they did. This probably isn't the time to get into it, though."

"Yeah, fair enough," Shepherd said. He looked at Cross and saw the growing impatience on the Lieutenant Commander's face. "Sorry about that, Commander. Just caught me a little off guard is all."

"No harm done," Cross said. To Lancaster he said, "Welcome, Sergeant. Have a seat."

"Thank you, Sir," Lancaster said.

To bring the team up to speed, Cross laid out a brief overview of Staff Sergeant Lancaster's background and qualifications. According to his research and interviews, Lancaster had joined the Air Force just before the Pentagon had removed the ban on women serving in combat roles in the US military. The ban had been an official Department of Defense rule since only the mid-1990s despite being an ongoing military tradition long before that. But with the most recent wars in Iraq and Afghanistan, women in supposedly non-combat roles were being put in exactly the same danger as their male fellow-soldiers. After a time, it became clear just how senseless and sexist the rule had been.

When the Secretary of Defense finally lifted the restriction, Lancaster was among the first wave of women who sought to push even further into the male-only special operations sector. While most of the military engaged in endless debates and bureaucratic foot-dragging, the Air Force's Combat Control quietly opened its admissions to women who were willing to meet its program's high physical and mental standards. Lancaster had been one of the select few women who made it all the way from the Combat Control Selection Course to Combat Control School. In short order, she earned her level-three ranking as a combat controller.

Afterward, Lancaster was ushered through the Special Tactics Advanced Skills Training courses. She quickly learned free-fall parachuting and combat diving, among other specialized skills. Throughout the process, she earned some of the best scores and ratings in the past decade. Some of her scores were even better than Brighton's had been.

Cross described Lancaster's recent deployments and the medals she had won for her exemplary service. What he left out, however, was a revelation Lancaster had made in her last interview: being part of his team was not her ideal career move. Were it up to her, she would have continued her training until she became the Air Force's first female officer — not just an operative.

In other words, she wants my job, Cross immediately realized. And he couldn't blame her for her frustration. As progressive as the Air Force had been thus far, Lancaster found her progress stifled. The process of selection at the Special Tactics Officer level was a series of interviews with older, long-serving officers. Sadly, none of them had shown the slightest interest in considering her for the officer program. While it was easier for the Air Force to move forward with integrating its male and female combatants, expecting the same progressive attitude from every individual was a dream yet to be realized.

All the same, Lancaster gladly accepted Cross's offer to join the team. Her sense of duty, Cross had come to realize, was greater than her specific career aspirations. The team needed her exceptional skills and dedication. And after all, Shadow Squadron did valuable work outside the cumbersome restrictions of the greater military bureaucracy. To Cross, it didn't matter whether that work was done by a man or woman as long as the soldier in question was skilled enough to get the job done. Lancaster was that sort of soldier, Cross believed.

"Welcome to Shadow Squadron, Sergeant," Cross said after he wrapped up the brief career and training history for the others.

"Hoo-rah," the men said in unison, echoing the sentiment.

Lancaster nodded, looking far more relaxed than she had when she'd first entered. She took her seat, and Cross began to lay out the extensive cohesion training to come.

* * *

Shepherd, Walker, and Cross were the last to leave the briefing room when the meeting was over. The soldiers had the next couple of hours to themselves, and Lancaster had been dismissed down to Supply to get her new equipment and speak to the tailor about her Shadow Squadron uniform. The standard Air Force uniform she'd worn in the field had been cut for a male body and didn't fit her quite right. One of the benefits of being part of Shadow Squadron was having a distinct field uniform that was also specifically tailored to each individual.

Shepherd was lingering by the door. "Say,

Commander, Chief?" he said to Walker and Cross. "Can I ask you something about Morgan?"

"Speak your mind, Sergeant," Cross said.

"Did you know we knew each other?" Shepherd said. "Me and Morgan."

"We didn't know about you and her sister," Walker answered. He'd helped Cross narrow his candidate selection to replace Brighton down to three. After that, he recommended Lancaster above the other two applicants. "I saw you went to the same high school at the same time, though. As small as your graduating class was, it seemed likely you'd met at least."

"That doesn't have anything to do with why you picked her, does it?" Shepherd asked. "Did you think that maybe since I knew her that'd make it easier for the other guys to accept her?"

"The thought crossed my mind," Walker admitted.

"Well, do me a favor, Chief," Shepherd said. "Don't tell her that."

"Don't worry, Sergeant," Cross said. "This team

doesn't need a kid sister or a mascot. It needs a good soldier who can do the work. Lancaster's proven to the Chief and me that she's legit, and I'm fully confident she can prove the same to you and the others on her own. Without your help."

Shepherd nodded. "Good. I'm glad to hear you say that, Sir," he said. "Lord knows I already have enough sisters of my own to worry about back home."

Walker frowned. "I'm willing to bet your sisters worry about you even more," he said.

Shepherd paused. "Fair enough," he said with a nod.

5514.108

INTEL

DECRYPTING

12345

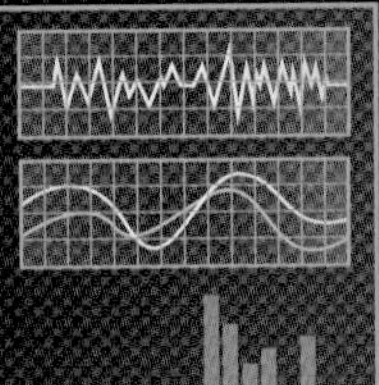

COM CHATTER

- DRONE: an unmanned aircraft or ship that can be navigated by remote control
- RANSOM: money paid to a kidnapper or hostage-taker for the safe release of said hostage
- SURVEILLANCE: a watch kept over a person, especially over a suspect

3245.98

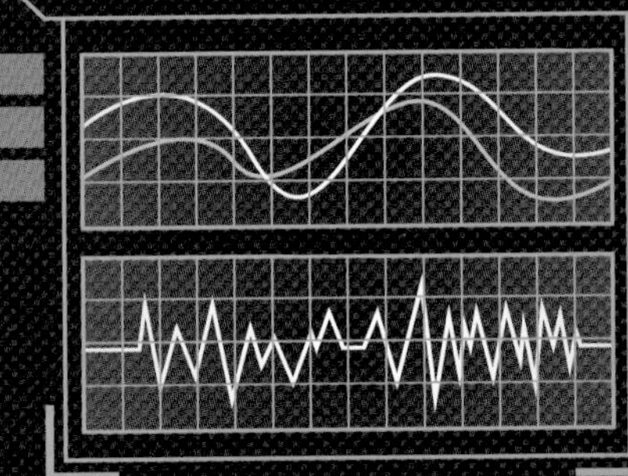

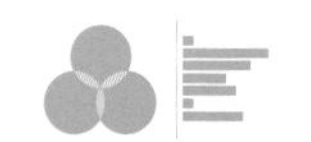

CHAPTER TWO

INTERRUPTION

Two weeks into Shadow Squadron's cohesion training, Cross called an unexpected meeting in the briefing room. He saw confusion on every face as the team filed in — even Chief Walker's. Cross couldn't tell if they could read his own aggravation and frustration in his features, but he hoped not.

"Change of plans," he said when everyone was seated. Fortunately, he didn't add "gentlemen" this time, which he'd been doing for most of the past two weeks whenever he addressed the group. *Little victories,* he thought. "We've got a priority mission that puts cohesion training on hold for now. Word just came through this morning. From high up."

"How high?" Chief Walker asked. "Command tends to give us our space during training."

"True," Cross said. He took a deep breath to stifle a frustrated sigh. "But Command's hands are tied on this one. By the purse strings."

"Oh," Walker said, reading between the lines. Lieutenant Kimiyo Yamashita, an Army Ranger and the team's sniper, nodded knowingly as well. The others looked confused.

"I've been on the phone half the night with Senator Jason Barron," Cross explained. "For those of you who don't know, he's the head of the sub-committee that controls our little program's secret budget." With that, all remaining confusion vanished from around the table.

"Yesterday afternoon," Cross said, "Senator Barron received this voicemail."

Cross tapped the touchpad on the table. Instantly, a scratchy and static-garbled voice came from the room's speakers.

CLICK.

"Dad, it's Jack . . . Temedt office in Tessalit . . . have to help . . . I told them about my trust fund . . . by wire in one week . . . bad connection . . . week."

"That's it?" Walker asked after the recording ended.

"It's all the Senator's technicians could make out," Cross said.

"It's authentic?" Walked asked.

"Senator Barron is sure it's his son's voice, but the original recording is even worse than this one. It tracks, though. His son's been in Mali — which is where the city of Tessalit is — since he graduated college. He's been working with this Temedt group in an effort to raise awareness of slavery over there."

"So Barron's worried something's happened to his son?" Staff Sergeant Adam Paxton asked.

Chief Walker nodded. "He probably doesn't like the sound of 'have to help,'" he said.

"That's exactly it," Cross said. "The Senator doesn't know any details, but he believes his son is in some sort of danger. Specifically, he's convinced himself that Jack's been kidnapped. Likely by some group of slavers the local Temedt office has gone up against. Jack has a trust fund set up by his grandfather, and Senator Barron believes the fact that his son mentioned it indicates there's a ransom demand involved here."

"But he isn't certain," Yamashita said flatly.

"Right," Cross said. "Neither the son nor any alleged kidnappers have been back in contact with him since. So they came to us."

"So what's the Senator want from us?" Shepherd asked.

"He wants our boots on the ground," Cross said. "We're to get into Mali, find and rescue his son, and bring him back home."

"Assuming he's been kidnapped," Paxton said.

"Assuming he's even still alive," Yamashita added.

"Right," Cross said again, his voice grim. "Should that not be the case, we're to 'find, root out, and punish the evildoers.' The Senator's words, not mine."

"Why us?" Paxton asked.

"Fair question," Cross said. "As the Senator explains it, no other team has the proper motivation to see this done as well and quickly as we do."

Cross saw his expression of distaste mirrored in the faces around the table. Yamashita broke the silence that had fallen.

"Meaning that Senator Barron is prepared to hold our budget hostage so we'll do what he wants," Yamashita said. "Ironic."

"Yeah," Cross said. "Very ironic."

"To think I voted for that guy," Lancaster muttered.

Walker looked up at Lancaster. For a moment, Cross expected him to growl a warning at Lancaster the way he always had whenever Brighton used to make smart remarks. Instead, the Chief burst out laughing. The others joined in as well, trading surprised looks around the table. Even Yamashita chuckled, which was a rarity all on its own. Lancaster scratched the back of her neck self-consciously and looked up at Cross with an apologetic shrug.

"All right, all right," Cross said. "Settle down. We have a trip and a blind operation to plan. And if the Senator's deductions are accurate, we've got less than a week to pull this thing off."

As the laughter died off and professionalism kicked in, Cross activated the table's touchpad once again. The overhead projector whirred to life. A world map appeared on the whiteboard, and Cross walked over to it. He touched a light stylus to Mali up in the northwest of Africa. Another tap broke the Mali map into its eight administrative regions, and Cross selected one of the two regions in the eastern portion.

"This is the Kidal Region," he said, centering it on the display. "In 2011, Tuareg and Islamist rebels tried to turn the entire northern half of Mali, including Kidal, into an independent region called Azawad. The Malian government's was losing ground there, but then began taking it back by degrees with the French military's aid. Meanwhile, the Tuaregs have been fighting the Islamists as the Islamists have been trying to lay down sharia law in the region. US forces have been on the sidelines monitoring the Islamists for any connections that might arise to Al-Qaeda or other terrorist groups."

Lancaster nodded at that last part. She'd most recently been stationed across the eastern border in Niger as part of that effort, as well as to lend occasional aid to French forces active in Mali.

"Long story short," Cross continued, "it's a mess over there. The local armies on both sides of the conflict are a shambles, and law enforcement is iffy at best. And the farther north you go, the deeper you get into the desert, which means communities are smaller and farther apart. Very Wild West. Slavery is an issue as well. It's against local law, but it also has a strong historical and traditional backbone. Organizations like this Temedt group that the Senator's son mentioned are doing what they can to combat it, but the farther you get from solid government control, the harder it is to wipe out.

Cross touched his stylus to the whiteboard once more, indicating the western half of Kidal. "This district in the middle of the mess is Tessalit Cercle," he said.

Cross tapped again, narrowing down the scope of the display further. "This is Tessalit itself, the rural commune at the center of the district. Most of the greater area is either desert plains or part of the Adrar des Ifoghas mountain range; the commune is at an oasis in the mountains. This is Jack Barron's last known location. According to his own social media updates, he moved out there from Timbuktu last June. Our intelligence suggests that the mountain badlands of Adrar des Ifoghas are home to scattered camps of rebels fleeing Malian and French forces."

Cross took a breath and paused before continuing the briefing. The next part would be a tricky aspect of the mission, and he wanted to make sure he emphasized this next part. "If there are slaver groups operating in the area, they could be hiding there just as well," he said. "We'll start our investigation here and borrow some recon time from satellite flyovers and the drones we have on station in Niger to help us keep an eye over the mountains. Command's already arranging for the satellite time. Lancaster, you'll be on point arranging the drone surveillance."

"Sir," Lancaster said.

"There's not much else to say at this point that we can't go over in flight," Cross said. "This is a blind operation with a tight deadline. We'll have more information on local contacts and a full aerial recon picture by the time we arrive. After that, all we can do is wait and see and react. So get your gear. We've got an hour before our first flight takes off."

5514.108

INTEL

DECRYPTING

12345

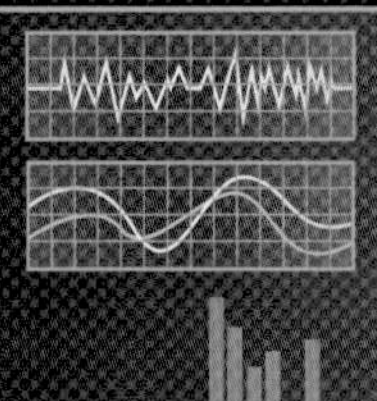

COM CHATTER

- CV-22B OSPREY: an American tiltrotor aircraft capable of vertical landings and ascents
- FAMAS BULLPUP: a French-made assault rifle capable of fully automatic fire
- M1161 GROWLER: a durable but lightweight military vehicle designed to be transported by Osprey aircraft

3245.98

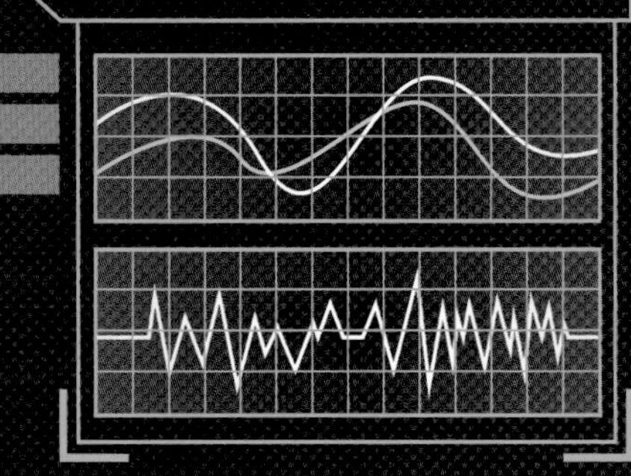

CHAPTER THREE

1324.014

OUTREACH

In no time at all, the team gathered its gear and boarded two of its state-of-the-art CV-22B Ospreys for the long trip to Mali. The Osprey could take off and land like a standard airplane or vertically like a helicopter. With its extended range and additional wing fuel tanks, the Osprey was able to cross the Atlantic and make it all the way to Africa in one uninterrupted flight, slowing only for in-flight refueling.

That's not to say the ride was a particularly comfortable one. The flight crew, half of Shadow Squadron, and half the team's gear filled much of each Osprey. In addition, each cargo compartment carried an M1161 Growler. The vehicle was a light utility, light strike, fast attack model much like a Jeep, but slimmer and with less armor. With so much space in use, standing room was at a premium. It was all the soldiers could do to get up and stretch their limbs during the long, monotonous voyage.

Shadow Squadron actually touched ground first in Niger after a fast flyover of Mali. The trip added their planes' own forward-looking infrared radar imagery to the growing cache of aerial reconnaissance Cross and Lancaster had arranged for. The Ospreys set down at the small airfield that Lancaster had helped set up when she'd been assigned there by the Air Force. A handful of technicians crawled over the aircraft like ants to check for signs of wear and tear after the long flight. They also removed the modular extra fuel tanks, refueled the regular tanks, and spot-checked the formidable armaments. By the time the checkup was finished, the Ospreys had been subtly transformed from long-haul workhorses to sleek, short-range birds of prey. The team then climbed back in to head west into Mali.

"You didn't want to catch up with your old pals?" Shepherd asked Lancaster once their Osprey was airborne again. The combat controller had spent most of the brief layover fiddling with the special gear she'd packed for the trip. "You were stationed here, right?"

"That was almost two years ago," Lancaster said. "All the guys I worked with have rotated out to other assignments. Besides, what could I even tell them about my new job?"

Cross overheard that and nodded grimly to himself. It was a hard fact of military life that the more elite and specialized a soldier became, the harder it became to relate to those soldiers outside one's immediate team or others at the same level of specialization. And it didn't get more specialized than the black-level secrecy under which Shadow Squadron operated. Lancaster didn't seem especially troubled by what she said, merely a little wistful, but Cross made a mental note to bring up the topic after cohesion training.

In no time at all, the Ospreys touched down at a

raggedy, all-but-deserted airstrip on the fringe of the Tessalit commune. When the Growlers were unloaded and Shadow Squadron had divided its personnel and gear into them, Cross gave the Osprey pilots their orders and led the expedition into Tessalit. The first stop would be the local Temedt office. Cross had been unable to make any sort of contact with the office by phone while en route. He hoped an in-person visit would prove more fruitful.

The office, when they finally found it, was nothing to write home about. It was a plain, brown, and square stone building that looked just like the ones to either side and across the street. Inside, a teenage girl doggedly pedaled a stationary bike connected by belts to the ceiling fans that did nothing to cool the air but at least kept it circulating. She spoke neither English nor French, but Chief Walker spoke in Bambara and learned that the head of operations was in his office at the rear of the building.

The head of operations made no secret that he was not pleased to see soldiers in his office, but he told Cross what he wanted to know. Jack Barron and his partner, a local man named Pierre Sanogo, were on a charity outreach mission in a distant village named Cadran Solaire. The Temedt officer was surprised that Barron might have been kidnapped, claiming he'd heard nothing of the sort. Barron hadn't checked in yet this week, but he wasn't expected back in Tessalit before Saturday. The Temedt officer offered to arrange a place for Cross and his soldiers to stay if they wanted to wait until then, but Cross declined. All Cross wanted was a location, directions, and local maps to compare against his own. When he got those, the team set out again.

An hour later, the Growlers pulled into Cadran Solaire. It was a modest collection of small, square, one-story stone buildings nestled into the crook of a sandstone valley with a single narrow pass on the far side. In one corner of the valley lay a deep, still pond of fresh water. A crooked spear of wind-smoothed stone rose out from the water as tall as a pine tree. Twelve round, flat rocks had been placed around the edge of the pond in a circle, each carved with Roman numerals representing the hours of the day. It was easily the biggest sundial Cross had ever seen.

A gang of some dozen children played soccer

in the dusty street. As Shadow Squadron pulled in, they all stopped to stare, blocking the Growlers' path. They crowded around the vehicles, chattering excitedly in Bambara, speaking to the soldiers as if they expected them to understand their language. Cross had no idea what they were saying, but he did catch a few words: Légion étrangère in French. He cut his Growler's engine and signaled for Chief Walker to do the same. They stepped out, leaving their vehicles where they stood.

"We're looking for Jack Barron," Cross told the assembled crowd in heavily accented French. "Or maybe Pierre Sanogo. They're from Temedt."

Walker repeated the question in Bambara. As the name penetrated the crowd, a chill seemed to settle on the kids. They became strangely reserved and took hold of the soldiers' hands to pull them toward the village.

The procession filed into the village past a few wary-looking adults standing in front of their homes in the shade of makeshift awnings. A man in a loose, sleeveless robe met them halfway. He greeted them politely enough but asked them bluntly why they'd come. When Walker told the man who they were looking for, the man backed off without a word and let the children continue leading the way.

When the kids finally gave way, they were at a building near the narrow canyon that led out the far side of the village. A Jeep larger and heavier than Shadow Squadron's Growlers sat parked outside it. The Jeep had a heavy machine gun mounted on the back. Two men in Malian army uniforms without rank or company insignia lounged against the Jeep, chatting in low tones. When Cross and then Walker tried to ask who the men were, the children either pretended ignorance or acted like they didn't see anyone. They were adamant that Barron and Sanogo were inside the building, however, so Cross and Walker thanked them and sent them back off to play. The kids merely retreated to a safe distance to see what would happen next.

"Chief, with me," Cross said, nodding toward the building. "Everybody else, keep an eye out."

With Walker behind him, Cross went in to find

Jack Barron. The building was someone's home, he found. A low table, washbasin, and clay oven dominated the main area. A sleeping area lay sectioned off behind a ratty cotton curtain. Seated at the table in the main room was a hard, muscular man in plain fatigues like those on the men by the Jeep. A FAMAS bullpup rifle stood leaning against the table in arm's reach. Across from him sat a local man in civilian clothes and a foreigner who could only be Jack Barron.

Barron looked quite different from the clean-shaven college kid in his father's reference photos. Gone were the polo shirt and chinos and the sixty-dollar haircut. Now he wore a faded cloth shirt over khaki cargo pants. His sun-bleached hair hung down past his ears in limp, disordered curls. His skin had been baked earthenware brown everywhere except around his eyes and in two bars over his ears. The skin there was still mushroom-stalk white from his overprotective eyewear. His arms were skinny like a monkey's and his long-fingered hands couldn't seem to stay at rest, even in the moment of surprise when Cross and Walker entered.

"Jack Barron?" Cross said, pointedly ignoring the other men. "US military. Got a minute?"

"Aww, man," Barron groaned. "My dad sent you, didn't he?"

INTEL

DECRYPTING

12345

COM CHATTER

- GREEN BERET: special forces (soldiers) from the US Army
- M4 CARBINE: a lightweight and compact assault rifle capable of fully automatic fire
- SLAVER: a dealer or trader of slaves or slave labour

3245.98

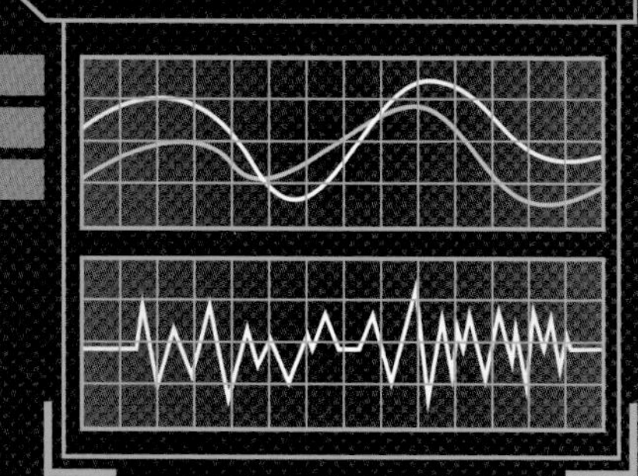

CHAPTER FOUR

ALTERCATION

"Well, clearly I haven't been kidnapped," Barron said, as if he were explaining things to an idiot. "Didn't my father tell you?"

Cross, Walker, and Barron had stepped out of the house and were huddled off to one side speaking in low tones. Barron's partner, Pierre Sanogo, and the man in fatigues remained inside to continue their business. Jannati and Yamashita waited by the door of the house while the rest of Shadow Squadron milled about waiting for orders. Shepherd seemed to be locked in a staring contest with one of the men guarding the armed Jeep.

"Your father wasn't very clear on your condition," Cross said through his teeth. "He neglected to tell us he spoke to you after that voicemail you sent him."

"Weird," Barron said. "Why would he do that?"

"I'd love to know," Cross said. "What did you two talk about?"

"Work," Barron said, maybe too quickly. "And my trust fund. Mostly that."

"What about it?" Walker asked. Cross remembered that Barron had mentioned the trust fund in his voicemail as well.

"I was trying to get Dad to give me some money out of it," Barron said. "My grandfather's will makes him the trustee, but I'm supposed to be able to decide how the money gets spent. Until I turn 25, though, I can't get any money without my dad's approval."

"What did you want it for?" Walker asked.

"Work," Barron said quickly, breaking eye contact. "You know, work-related stuff."

"Let me guess," Cross said. "You want to donate it to Temedt."

"Yeah," Barron said. "You know, for the cause and all that."

"But he wouldn't okay it?" Cross asked. Barron shook his head. Cross added, "And what happened when he told you that? I imagine you argued."

"More than that," Barron said. "I told him I was going to call my lawyer. If my cell phone hadn't died, I would have done it right then. As it is, I'll have to wait 'til Saturday when Pierre and I are back in Tessalit."

"You're not going to have to wait," Cross said. "We've got a sat-phone. Once I get off line with Command, you, me, and your father are going to have a little talk. Chief, keep an eye on him."

Cross stalked away to make the call to Command, leaving Walker and Barron alone. While he waited for the computer to recognize his voice and access code, he listened to Walker and Barron talk.

"I don't get this," Barron was saying. "Is your captain ticked at me?"

"He's not a captain," Walker said. "And it's not

you. If there's anybody who's going to get an earful, it's your father. He pulled some pretty important strings to send us racing over here to rescue you from trouble he knew you weren't actually in. Senator or no, your father's going to have to answer for that."

You got that right, Cross thought. He kept his voice relatively calm and professional when he got his Command contact on the line, but he insisted that Command conference in the Senator without delay. He smiled grimly when the Command operator put him on hold to contact Senator Barron's office.

Before he could get the Senator on the line, a commotion demanded his attention and he had to hang up. Shouts in English, French, and Bambara erupted from the house where they'd found Barron. One of the voices belonged to Lieutenant Jannati, whom Cross had sent to keep an eye on things by the door. When Cross looked over, neither Yamashita nor Jannati were where he'd left them, and the other members of his team were stirring themselves to confused action by the door.

Cross had taken no more than a step in that

direction himself when the man who'd been meeting with Barron and Sanogo staggered backward out the door and fell on his backside in the dusty street. Jannati emerged a second later and kicked the man in the back as he tried to roll away. Yamashita and Pierre Sanogo came out next. Sanogo looked horrified and reached out to pull Jannati back from the man on the ground, but Yamashita stopped Sanogo with a firm hand in the center of his chest. The sniper's eyes scanned from Jannati to the man on the ground and then over to the Jeep the man had arrived in. He cocked an eyebrow at what he saw, then looked over at Shepherd.

Cross then saw what the sniper had seen. The two men who'd been guarding the Jeep were scrambling into action, hurriedly yanking the FAMAS rifles slung over their shoulders into their hands. Fortunately, Paxton and Shepherd saw the same thing. Stepping apart, they raised their M4 carbines and barked sharp orders for the two men to stand down. Hospital Corpsman Second Class Kyle Williams followed suit when he saw what the two Green Berets were doing. Lancaster hesitated, looking from Jannati to Cross

and then back to the two FAMAS-armed men before raising her weapon. The two Jeep guards stopped and pointed their rifles at the dirt, glancing at each other uncertainly.

Jannati drove another kick into the downed but still squirming man's ribs. The Malian yelped but remained on his knees.

"Lieutenant!" Cross yelled at Jannati. "Stand down, soldier!"

Jannati backed away just slightly out of kicking range, but his face was still a mask of rage.

Chief Walker ordered the two Jeep guards in Bambara to drop their weapons. He held his weapon across his chest and stood in front of Jack Barron, shielding him in case bullets started flying.

Finding themselves outgunned, the Jeep guards lay down their weapons and then backed off. Shepherd looked at Lancaster and nodded toward the weapons. She gathered them up and carried them over to Cross.

Cross stalked toward Jannati and stopped

opposite the man Jannati had kicked. "Explain yourself," Cross said firmly.

"Let this one explain it," Jannati said, throwing an accusatory glare at Pierre Sanogo. He gave a second one to Barron. "Or maybe the fortunate son over there."

"I said explain yourself," Cross growled, staring Jannati in the eye.

Jannati gritted his teeth, but Cross could tell the Marine wasn't angry with him. Jannati took a deep breath to compose himself, but the look of outrage returned when he glanced at the Malian at his feet.

"I overheard this piece of work talking in there while you and the Senator's kid were outside," Jannati began. "He's a slaver thug. He was trying to extort money from Temedt to leave this village alone. He's running a protection racket."

Although he wasn't as worked up as Jannati, Yamashita nodded his confirmation with a cold, faraway look in his eyes.

Cross heard Barron suck in a horrified breath.

Sanogo looked similarly stricken, but he only hung his head, the shame in his eyes failing to deny the accusation. Neither man looked surprised by Jannati's revelation but rather dismayed that the secret had come out in front of other people.

"So you just decided to go cowboy justice on him?" Cross demanded. "This isn't why we're here, Lieutenant."

Jannati couldn't have looked more surprised if Cross had slapped him. "Sir, I—"

"Quiet! I don't care what this two-bit lowlife's up to. He's not the mission." Cross pointed at Barron, who flinched as if Cross had pointed a weapon at him. "He's the mission. And frankly, I'm getting to the point where I don't care what happens to him, either."

Barron gulped. Jannati winced. Cross pressed on.

"Now take Mister Sanogo back in the house," he said. He made a gesture taking in Jannati and Yamashita. "I want the pair of you to keep an eye on him, but keep your hands to yourself. You read me?"

"Sir," Yamashita said. Jannati said the same, though it took him a few seconds to compose himself enough to say so.

"And you," Cross said in French to the Malian half-crouched in the dirt. "You understand me? Get up."

The Malian did so, glaring at Cross with plain hatred. Blood oozed from a swollen lip, and he clutched his side with one arm, breathing heavily. Bruised ribs, probably. "I don't care who you are or what you're doing here," Cross told the man. "Get your men, get in your Jeep, and get lost. I don't want to see you again before we fly out of here."

The Malian's eyes narrowed but he nodded. He hobbled over to his comrades, who looked just as helpless and defeated as he did.

"Sergeant," Cross said to Lancaster without taking his eyes off the wounded Malian. "Go make sure there's nothing else in their Jeep that we don't want there."

Lancaster tilted her head at the odd way Cross had worded the order. She paused for a moment but

then nodded and did as told. She left the two FAMAS rifles on the ground near Cross. When she reached the Jeep, Cross called out to the three Malians in French again.

"Hey, look at me," he called. "We're keeping these guns. I'm sure you've got more back home, but I strongly suggest you don't bring them back here."

The Malians grumbled and frowned at that but were in no position to protest. When Lancaster finished with their vehicle, she backed off to let the Malians clamber into it. They piled in and peeled out, tearing off through the sandstone canyon in a cloud of dust. Cross looked around to make sure his people were all right. He noticed that all of the locals had scattered into hiding. *Probably for the best,* Cross thought.

"What did you just do?" Barron asked in a scared, small voice. "You have no idea who that is."

"Let me guess," Cross replied, "that's why you actually wanted your trust fund. Protection money."

"Not that it matters now," Barron moaned.

"You told your father as much?" Cross continued.

"I tried to explain how things work over here," Barron said, "but he just said, 'You don't negotiate with these people, son. It only emboldens them.'"

"He's got a point," Cross said. "The more money you give people like that, the more they're going to want. Eventually they're going to bleed you dry if you don't stand up to them."

"That's easy for you to say," Barron said. "You don't live here. Plus, you've got the Army behind you. What do these people have? Not much against that guy you just humiliated in front of all of them. Do you know who he even is? His name's Bubaga, but the locals call him the Spider. He's not just some slave broker. He runs guns to the Islamists and the Tuaregs all over Azawad. He does protection rackets and human trafficking over three regions. He's got an entire army he formed from rebel deserters and mercenaries the government couldn't afford to pay anymore. Bubaga is a dangerous man, but for all that, he's at least honorable. He respects money, and I've got more than plenty to spare. I could've handled this if you hadn't interfered."

"Except you don't have that money," Cross said. "Your father wouldn't sign off on it, right? If you told him what you're doing here and who you're dealing with, that's probably why he sent us out here. He didn't want you to have to deal with Bubaga when you couldn't deliver the money you promised."

"I could've explained things," Barron said, though without confidence.

"Unlikely," Walker said, returning. He looked at Cross and said, "Ospreys are on the way, Sir."

"What's an Osprey?" Barron asked.

"It's our ride," Cross said. "And yours too, if you want it."

"What? You're just . . . leaving?"

"Yep," Cross said. "Full of sound and fury. As far as I'm concerned, this mission's over. You're accounted for and free, so my team's done. You're welcome to fly out with us, of course, but you're not obligated. You're a grown man."

"Bubaga is coming back here, you know," Barron said. "You understand that, right? He's going to wait until he sees you leave, then he's going to come back with his men to take out what you did to him on these people. Don't you think you have a responsibility to deal with that? Especially since one of yours caused the problem in the first place?"

"What I think is that I'm getting my people in the air when our ride gets here," Cross said. "You can go with us or you can stay here. Choice is yours."

"Fine then!" Barron spat. "Go! But I'm not abandoning these people. You can go home if you want, but good luck explaining to my father what you're letting happen."

Cross turned away without a word, signaling to Walker. The two of them walked away to gather up the men, collect the Growlers, and wait for the Ospreys to take them away from Cadran Solaire.

5514.108

INTEL

DECRYPTING

12345

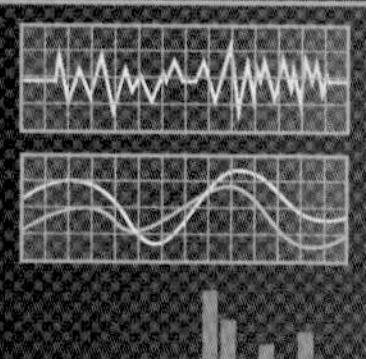

COM CHATTER

- .50 CAL: a heavy-duty bullet used in larger machine guns
- AMBUSH: the act of lying concealed in order to surprise an enemy
- OVERWATCH: a small unit that helps observe the battlefield
- TRACKER: a device that tracks the location of something or someone

3245.98

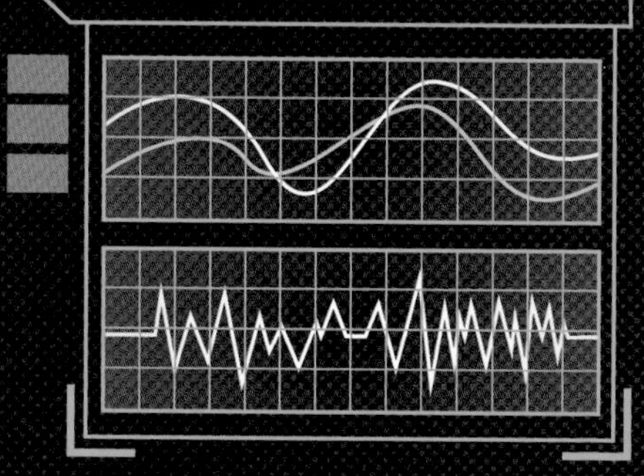

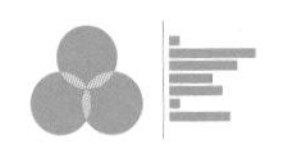

CHAPTER FIVE

ADAPTATION

The team's Ospreys traversed the darkening Malian sky. "Speak your mind, Lieutenant," Cross said to Jannati, who hadn't said a word since the Ospreys had arrived in Cadran Solaire. Also on his Osprey were Lancaster and Yamashita. The other Osprey carried Walker, Shepherd, Paxton and Williams. Lancaster sat hunched over her laptop computer, the glow from the screen illuminating her face.

"We can't just leave them there, Commander," Jannati said. He was no longer scowling or frowning, but he still didn't look happy. "Those people have no idea what this guy is going to do to them."

"I agree completely, Lieutenant," Cross said. He'd spent the first several minutes of the flight getting back in touch with Command to request any available intelligence on this Bubaga character Jannati had pummeled and humiliated. The file Command had sent back read like something out of a comic book villain's biography. Bubaga's wartime atrocities were almost as bad as the crimes Bubaga's own criminal gang had wrought against the civilians who defied him.

"That's why we're not leaving," Cross said.

Jannati blinked. "I beg your pardon, Sir?"

"If we were just turning tail and going home, we could've driven the Growlers back to the air field," Cross explained. "Bringing the Ospreys in and dusting off like we did was all for show. I wanted Bubaga to see us leaving and think the village is undefended."

"You're sure he was watching?" Jannati asked dubiously.

"Lancaster?" Cross said, looking at the combat controller.

"His Jeep stopped about half a mile outside Cadran Solaire and waited there until we'd lifted off and were out of sight," Lancaster said, looking up from her laptop. "He took up his original heading after that. I'll let you know when he stops again."

Jannati looked at Lancaster, clearly confused.

"I put a tracker on his car when I was pretending to search it for weapons," Lancaster told him. "Well, I searched it too. But I also placed the tracker."

Cross was pleased Lancaster had read his implied instructions without needing them spelled out.

"So we're going back to the village?" Jannati asked, relieved.

"No," Cross said. "We're going to assume this guy's coming back there as soon as he gets to his hideout, rearms, and gathers his men. We're going to set down in his path and intercept him. If we do this right, the villagers shouldn't be aware of what's going on until it's already over."

Cross rose and activated the high-definition teleconference screen mounted on the wall. On it appeared a cargo-bay view of the other Osprey as seen from the perspective of its own teleconference screen. Walker was visible on-screen, and the other three soldiers with him were gathered around him.

"We're ready here, Sir," the Chief said. "Do we know where the target's headed yet?"

Cross looked at Lancaster. She swiped something from her laptop's touch-sensitive screen toward the Osprey's teleconference screen. A digital contour map of local terrain appeared on half of the screen. A blinking dot labeled with a radio frequency ID appeared, moving through a narrow path through the mountain. The dot represented the tracker Lancaster had hidden on Bubaga's car.

"The path he's on dead-ends into that mountain," Lancaster said. "I don't see any signs of a base, though. My best guess from available aerial recon is that it leads into a cave system or just a complex where he's settled his slaving network."

"Or a *web*," Walker said. "You know, because he's called the Spider." Cross stared blankly at Walker. "Sorry, Commander. Go ahead."

Cross finally allowed himself to grin. The Chief must miss Brighton — now he was the one chiming in with bad jokes.

"Anyway," Cross said. "I'm not keen to chase this guy and his mercenary thugs down into unfamiliar caves in the dead of night. Instead, we'll meet him halfway when he sets out for Cadran Solaire's blood."

Cross dragged his fingertips along the half of the teleconference screen showing the digital aerial map, moving the image backward along the path Bubaga's Jeep had taken.

"Here," he said. The part of the road he'd indicated cut a blind curve through a sandstone pass with a steep wall on the inner curve. There was a sharp, shorter embankment on the outer side. "Chief, you got it?"

Walker tapped his screen, making a blip appear on Cross's screen. "Got it."

"This is where we'll hit them. We'll park one of the Growlers here." Cross tapped the screen, leaving a bright dot on the map. "This'll be Attack One. If we can blow part of this rock wall down to block the road when they get there, that would be ideal. Lancaster, you and the Chief will assess the terrain."

"Sir," Walker and Lancaster replied.

"I want the other Growler here. This is Attack Two." He tapped the screen again. "If not, we'll have to put Attack Two here." One final tap. "Right around this blind curve where they won't see it until it's too late. I'm going to need a volunteer to man that gun."

"Yo," Shepherd said, raising his hand.

"It's yours, Sergeant," Cross told him with a grateful nod. Shepherd hadn't chosen the easy job. If Attack Two had to pull double-duty as a roadblock, it was going to be terribly exposed. Cross turned to Yamashita and indicated another area on the map that was near the ambush site. "Lieutenant, I was thinking here for overwatch. Is this close enough?"

"What's the scale on this map?" Yamashita asked.

"Oops, sorry," Lancaster said. She tapped a few keys on her laptop, and a scale measurement appeared in the bottom corner of the screen.

Yamashita peered at the screen. "It'll do."

"Good. Lancaster, once you set the explosives — or don't — you'll take Four-Eyes and go with Yamashita. You'll keep in constant contact with the Ospreys as well, on the off chance we need their firepower for support. I don't want you down in the soup on this one, though."

"Sir?" Lancaster asked, looking insulted or deeply disappointed.

"I'm not being chivalrous, Sergeant," Cross told her. "You haven't finished cohesion training with us yet. Until you do, you're on overwatch."

"Oh," Lancaster said with a quick nod. "Sir."

"Paxton, set up here at Cover One," Cross went on, indicating another section of the map, this one behind the ambush point. "If they try to run and get past us, you're the goalie."

"Sir."

"Williams, Cover Two's going to be here. Our gunners are going to be the most exposed when the shooting starts, so I want you to be where you can get to them fast. You've also got a partially covered route out to Cover One if Paxton's hit."

"Sir," the corpsman responded.

"Jannati, you'll be on the gun at Attack One."

"Hoo-rah," Jannati said, his eyes dancing.

"Chief, you and I will drive the Growlers into position and support the gunners."

"Sounds good," Walker said.

Without another word, Cross turned to go and give orders to the Ospreys' flight crews. Before he closed the cabin door behind him, he heard Lancaster turn and speak to Yamashita.

* * *

The sun had set when Bubaga's men set out for their intended retaliation against Cadran Solaire. The new moon sky glowed with a dusting of countless stars, and the sound of engines carried for miles through the darkness.

"They're coming, Commander," Lancaster said through her canalphone. From her vantage at overwatch, Lancaster was watching the road through the camera of the remote-controlled "Four-Eyes" quad-copter that Edgar Brighton had built.

Cross lay in the dirt at Attack One a few yards away from the Growler manned by Aram Jannati. His M4 carbine was propped on his half-empty backpack. His AN/PSQ-20 nightvision lens painted the ambush point in shades of bright green. "How many?" Cross asked.

"Five full Jeeps, one man each on the .50 cals," Lancaster reported. "There's an ACMAT truck behind them. It has a large cage on the back."

"Is it empty?" Cross asked.

"Yessir."

"Noted," Cross said. "Seems Bubaga intends to bring any survivors back to his base as slaves."

"That ACMAT could work to block the road behind the Jeeps," Yamashita said over the channel.

"Make it happen when we drop the roadblock in front," Cross said. "Cover One, move to Cover Two."

"Sir," Paxton replied. A moment later, he reported that he was at his new position.

Another few minutes after that, Lancaster reported that the Jeeps were right around the corner. Cross ordered his soldiers to get ready. The engine noise was right on top of them, and the Jeeps' headlights shone from around the blind corner. Cross lifted his nightvision lens so the headlights wouldn't blind him. "Contact. Roadblock ready."

"Ready, Sir," Lancaster said.

The first Jeep's headlights passed right under the high sandstone shelf where Cross and Jannati's Growler was perched. No one in the Jeep seemed to notice them waiting up there. Nor did they spot Attack Two ahead. Two more Jeeps rounded the corner. Then two more. The ACMAT came last.

"Close the road," Cross said.

"Sir," Lancaster said.

Cross looked away as the C4 plastic explosives exploded ahead of the Jeeps. The night shook with a heavy boom. Rocks the size of barrels tumbled into the road. A cloud of dust billowed out in all directions.

A second later, a muted crack sounded at the rear of the slaver convoy. Cross saw the windshield of the ACMAT shatter inward as Yamashita eliminated the driver with a silenced shot from his M110 sniper rifle. The truck nosed toward the edge of the road and coasted to a stop, blocking the way out. The five Jeeps were now trapped between it and the rockslide.

"Attack One, Attack Two," Cross said. "Go."

RAT-TAT-TAT-TAT-TAT!

RAT-TAT-TAT-TAT-TAT!

Jannati and Shepherd opened up with the Growler's guns, cutting into the first and last vehicles in the line. Jannati targeted the ACMAT's hood with a laser-accurate stream of 7.62x55mm NATO rounds from the minigun, blowing the engine to smithereens so no one could drive away. From farther up, Shepherd sprayed a second stream into the lead Jeep. The driver of that vehicle slammed on his brakes as Shepherd's bullets tore into the side of the vehicle and sent gouts of black smoke pouring from under its hood.

The Jeeps left in the middle lurched to a stop, and the men within reacted in a semi-coordinated panic. The second one backed up a few feet and made as if to try to maneuver around the smoking hulk of the first Jeep. Its headlights washed directly over Attack Two, illuminating Shepherd at the M134 and Walker in a shooter's crouch behind a rock. The third Jeep backed into the fourth, which was trying to move around to follow the second. The man at the fourth Jeep's machine gun fell off, and the third Jeep's gunner fired a burst in the air as he clung to the weapon for balance. The fifth Jeep remained where it was, and the men inside leaped out to return fire.

"Flares!" Cross called over the din.

"Sir!" Lancaster called over the canalphone.

FOOOSH! FOOOSH!

A second later, a set of magnesium lights lit up the desert night. The flares had been Lancaster's idea. Hidden on the road all along the ambush site and detonated by remote, they blazed to furious life among the startled would-be raiders. At such close quarters, the near light blinded the Malians and made their distant targets nearly impossible to see. From outside the immediate area of effect, the light illuminated the Malians perfectly, making them better targets.

"Fire at will," Cross said quietly.

Thunder shattered the night. Walker shot down the machine gunner on the destroyed lead Jeep. The gunner on the fifth Jeep tried to return fire on Attack One through the magnesium glare. Most of his shots were wide to the left, but Cross heard a few dig into the Growler's rear end. Jannati turned the M134 on him, cutting him down and shredding the vehicle. Those of the Jeep's occupants who'd made it out threw themselves flat, scrambling for cover behind the other vehicles.

Of the two Jeeps that had collided, only one gunner remained in position, and he swiveled his barrel up back toward Attack One. The gunner of the Jeep facing Attack Two opened up, spraying wildly. Some of the bullets tore into Walker's cover, forcing the Chief to dive out of the way cursing in Spanish. Fire from Shepherd's minigun knocked the shooter from the back of the Jeep.

Cross picked off the gunner between the two collided vehicles while Jannati fired on the rearmost of the two Jeeps to keep the gunner who'd fallen off from trying to reclaim his firing position. The gunner retreated toward what minimal cover he could find. Most of the passengers of the two collided Jeeps made it out unharmed, though a burst from Paxton's M4 from Cover Two caught the last one out before he could close the door.

"Frag out!" Williams called as Paxton's man slid to the ground, clinging weakly to the door of the Jeep. The corpsman hurled an M67 fragmentation grenade into the space between the rear bumper and grill of the two collided Jeeps. The blast made the vehicles jump apart and threw a hail of deadly steel fragments into the slavers hiding behind them.

"Suppressing fire," Cross ordered. "Attack Two, move down to flank."

"Sir," Walker replied.

BANG BANG BANG BANG BANG
BANG BANG BANG BANG
BANG BANG BANG BANG

As heavy fire from both miniguns ate away at the savaged Jeeps like starving wolves, Cross and Walker came down to road level from their cover positions at opposite ends of the ambush site. Cross came down behind the disabled ACMAT truck and put it between himself and his men. Walker came down along the inside of the fallen-stone roadblock and took cover behind the first Jeep. The magnesium flares were still burning, but thick smoke from the vehicles and brownish dust from the C4 explosion hung in the air, reducing visibility. Cross lifted his M4 to the ready and began to make his way forward.

"Oh, right, right," Lancaster said in Cross's canalphone, likely at some silent urging from Yamashita. "Sir, you've got . . . it looks like . . . seven left moving down there."

No sooner were the words out of Lancaster's mouth than the passenger door of the half destroyed Jeep nearest Cross fell off. A half-dead Malian lurched out with a bullpup FAMAS rifle clutched under one bleeding arm. His weapon was already trained on Cross as he dropped to one knee to take aim.

POP!

Yet, Yamashita was faster than them both. The sniper's bullet caught the man in the chest, dropping him at Cross's feet.

"Thanks," Cross said.

"Sir," Yamashita said.

"Make that eight," Lancaster said. "Well, now it's seven."

Cross smirked.

* * *

Between the crossfire and the suppressing fire from the team's attack and cover positions, the remaining men of Bubaga's band didn't stand a chance. Cross understood the grim necessity of the work, but it still sickened him. It was little comfort to think that these men had likely shown no mercy to the people they'd slaughtered or sold into slavery at Bubaga's command.

As for the so-called Spider, they found him laid out by the roadside near an outcropping of rock, a bullet hole in his chest.

"Looks like he was trying to skitter away," Walker said.

"Damage report," Cross said, allowing the bad joke. He was just glad the unpleasantness was done.

"Our Growler's not going anywhere," Jannati said. "The rear end's in a million pieces."

"We'll use the other one to push it onto its Osprey," Cross said. He turned to the team's corpsman. "Kyle?"

"No hits," Williams reported. "One injury. Very minor."

"Injury?" Shepherd said, waving a hand filled with sterile gauze pads. A bright, bloody line had cut his cheek below his left eye. Cross noticed it and cocked an eyebrow, waiting for an explanation. "A chip off the Chief's cover nicked me when they shot it up, Commander."

Cross nodded and turned away. He tapped his canalphone. "Overwatch, report."

"Clear," Yamashita said.

"Clear," Lancaster echoed. "I was about to bring Four-Eyes back here."

"Just land it here and reel in," Cross replied.

"Sir," Lancaster said.

"This was grim, ugly work, team," Cross said to

those assembled before him and over the canalphone. "But well done all the same."

He felt like he should say something else. Maybe something about the villagers they'd protected by what they'd done or something along those lines. But no words seemed to suit the situation. Instead, Cross simply nodded and turned away, switching channels on his canalphone to call the waiting Ospreys. When the call was made, Walker led him aside, looking down the road with a troubled expression.

"What's on your mind, Chief?" Cross asked.

"The base these ones came from," Walker said. "The mine, the cave . . . whatever it is. Bubaga could have more men down there."

"Maybe," Cross said.

"Or slave prisoners," Walker continued. He pointed at the ruined ACMAT. "The look of this truck makes me think he intended to round up the people of Cadran Solaire and bring them there. If he has a place to hold them . . ."

"He could already have other people there," Cross finished for him. "It's a possibility, but it's not the mission. Not our mission, anyway. Our mission's over."

Walker looked down the road, clearly not pleased to hear that.

"Tell you what, Chief," Cross said. "There's a Malian Army base not too far away in Amachach. We'll give them our intel on Bubaga's operation and tell them we got it by working off a tip from Jack Barron. We'll tell them what we did and let them take the credit for it as long as they promise to do two things in return."

"What two things?" Walker asked.

"First, they publicly give credit for the tip to Barron — a tireless Temedt crusader saving lives far from home. Second, they promise to get down here in force and deal with whatever's left in those caves."

Walker frowned. "You think they'll go along with that?" heasked.

"I think Command and I can impress on them the importance of going with the flow on this," Cross said with a smirk.

"I think that would qualify as a happy ending to this mess," the Chief said quietly. He looked up at the sound of distant rotors on the wind. "Ospreys are coming. Off to Amachach, then."

"First to Cadran Solaire," Cross corrected. "Barron needs to know the plan. I'm sure he'll be thrilled to know he's about to be a hero."

"His father too," Walker commented dryly. "Think how proud he'll be of his son, the hero."

"I look forward to reading all about it in the news when he breaks the story back home," Cross said.

"If the Senator plays his cards right, that story could win him the next election," Walker said.

Cross sighed. "So much for a happy ending, Chief."

Walker chuckled. "Sorry, Sir."

CLASSIFIED

MISSION DEBRIEFING

OPERATION

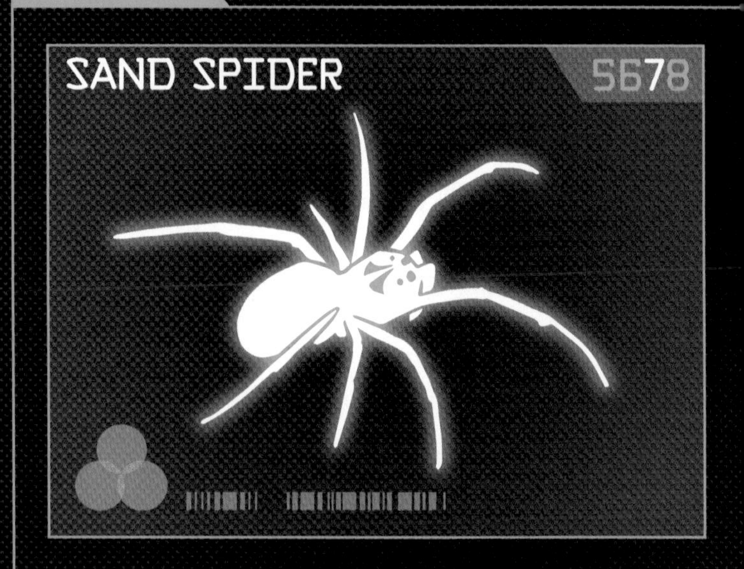

PRIMARY OBJECTIVES

- Determine location of hostage
- Escort hostage to safety

SECONDARY OBJECTIVES

x Avoid conflict with local forces

STATUS

2/3 COMPLETE

3245.98

CROSS, RYAN

RANK: Lieutenant Commander
BRANCH: Navy Seal
PSYCH PROFILE: Team leader of Shadow Squadron. Control oriented and loyal, Cross insisted on hand-picking each member of his squad.

I can't quite say this mission went off as originally planned. But with all things considered, I'm proud of our performance. We demonstrated the ability to think on our feet, and each of you showed you have the composure and adaptability necessary to be a part of Shadow Squadron. And we made Cadran Solaire a safer and better place.

Good job, everyone -- especially you, Lancaster. Welcome to the team.

- Lieutenant Commander Ryan Cross

ERROR

UNAUTHORIZED

USER MUST HAVE LEVEL 12 CLEARANCE OR HIGHER IN ORDER TO GAIN ACCESS TO FURTHER MISSION INFORMATION.

2019.681

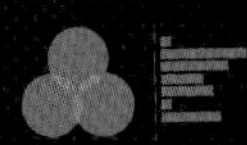

ARTIST

WILSON TORTOSA

Wilson "Wunan" Tortosa is a Filipino comic book artist best known for his works on *Tomb Raider* and the American relaunch of *Battle of The Planets* for Top Cow Productions. Wilson attended Philippine Cultural High School, then went on to the University of Santo Tomas where he graduated with a Bachelor's Degree in Fine Arts, majoring in Advertising.

COLORIST

BENNY FUENTES

Benny Fuentes lives in Villahermosa, Tabasco in Mexico, where the temperature is just as hot as the sauce. He studied graphic design in college, but now he works as a full-time colorist in the comic book and graphic novel industry for companies like Marvel, DC Comics, and Top Cow Productions. He shares his home with two crazy cats, Chelo and Kitty, who act like they own the place.

2019.681

CLASSIFIED

AUTHOR DEBRIEFING

CARL BOWEN

Q/When and why did you decide to become a writer?

A/I've enjoyed writing ever since I was in elementary school. I wrote as much as I could, hoping to become the next Lloyd Alexander or Stephen King, but I didn't sell my first story until I was in college. It had been a long wait, but the day I saw my story in print was one of the best days of my life.

Q/What made you decide to write *Shadow Squadron*?

A/As a kid, my heroes were always brave knights or noble loners who fought because it was their duty, not for fame or glory. I think the special ops soldiers of the US military embody those ideals. Their jobs are difficult and often thankless, so I wanted to show how cool their jobs are, but also express my gratitude for our brave warriors.

Q/What inspires you to write?

A/My biggest inspiration is my family. My wife's love and support lifts me up when this job seems too hard to keep going. My son is another big inspiration.

He's three years old, and I want him to read my books and feel the same way I did when I read my favorite books as a kid. And if he happens to grow up to become an elite soldier in the US military, that would be pretty awesome, too.

Q/Describe what it was like to write these books.

A/The only military experience I have is a year I spent in the Army ROTC. It gave me a great respect for the military and its soldiers, but I quickly realized I would have made a pretty awful soldier. I recently got to test out a friend's arsenal of firearms, including a combat shotgun, an AR-15 rifle, and a Barrett M82 sniper rifle. We got to blow apart an old fax machine.

Q/What is your favorite book, movie, and game?

A/My favorite book of all time is *Don Quixote*. It's crazy and it makes me laugh. My favorite movie is either *Casablanca* or *Double Indemnity*, old black-and-white movies made before I was born. My favorite game, hands down, is *Skyrim*, in which you play a heroic dragonslayer. But not even *Skyrim* can keep me from writing more *Shadow Squadron* stories, so you won't have to wait long to read more about Ryan Cross and his team. That's a promise.

BRIGHTON, EDGAR

RANK: Staff Sergeant
BRANCH: Air Force Combat Controller
PSYCH PROFILE: The team's technician and close-quarters-combat specialist is popular with his squadmates but often agitates his commanding officers.

LARSSEN, NEIL

RANK: Second Lieutenant
BRANCH: Army Ranger
PSYCH PROFILE: Neil prides himself on being a jack-of-all-trades. His versatility allows him to fill several roles for Shadow Squadron.

SHEPHERD, MARK

RANK: Lieutenant
BRANCH: Army (Green Beret)
PSYCH PROFILE: The heavy-weapons expert of the group, Shepherd's love of combat borders on unhealthy.

2019.681

CLASSIFIED

MISSION BRIEFING

OPERATION

We've just received a report that a Chinese oil rig platform in Cuban waters has been hijacked. Strangely, the hijackers are American mercenaries, and they've taken the workers hostage. To make matters worse, the Cuban military is on its way, and they have no concern for the lives of anyone on board. We can fully expect the Chinese military to intervene in short order, as well. If that happens, we'll have an international incident on our hands, and that's simply not an option. That means we need to get in, get the hostages, neutralize the mercs, and get out. Fast.

– Lieutenant Commander Ryan Cross

3245.98

PRIMARY OBJECTIVE(S)

- Secure the oil rig platform and transport hostages to safety

1932.789

SECONDARY OBJECTIVE(S)

- Minimize damage done to Hardwall mercenaries
- Avoid contact with the Cuban and Chinese forces

0412.981

1624.054

5514.108

INTEL

DECRYPTING

12345

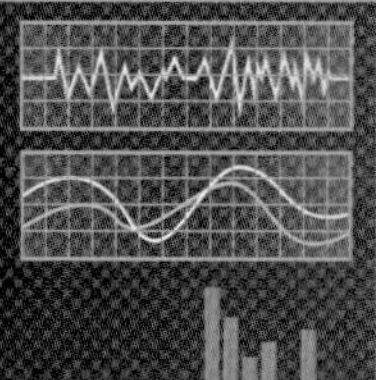

COM CHATTER

- BLACK OP – a black op, or operation, is a covert, secret mission
- REBREATHER – apparatus used to breathe under water
- NAVY SEAL – member of the Sea, Air, and Land teams that function as the US government's primary special operations force
- SDV – swimmer delivery vehicle, or a manned underwater submersible

3245.98

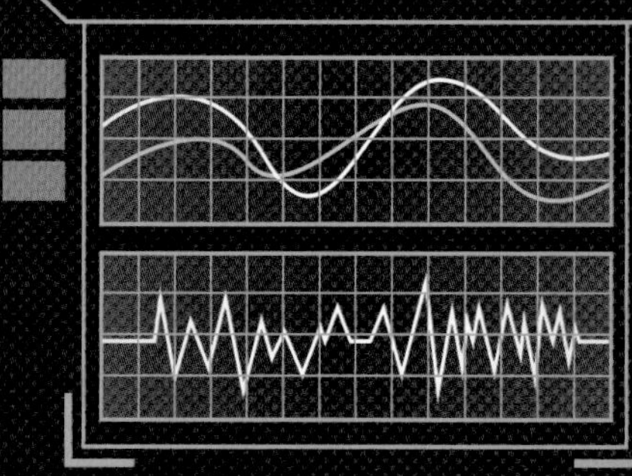

CHAPTER ONE

1324.014

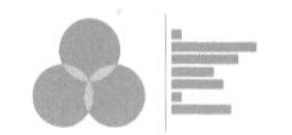

BLACK ANCHOR

The black salt water engulfed Chief Petty Officer Alonso Walker on all sides. He was in his element — both literally and figuratively. As a child, Walker had believed that the black depths of the ocean were filled with giant monsters like the Kraken, the Leviathan, and Moby Dick.

But now, as an adult, Walker knew there were few creatures in the sea more dangerous than himself. After all, he had been an elite career soldier of the US Navy. Now he was second-in-command of Shadow Squadron, and beside him floated a real, modern-day sea monster, the USS *Georgia*. It ws a 600-foot-long, Ohio-class nuclear submarine.

His present state had been a long time in the making. After coasting through twelve years of school with near perfect grades, Walker shocked his friends and family by enlisting in the Navy the day after graduation.

From the beginning, Walker had his sights set on joining the legendary SEALs. After a grueling trip through the SEAL training program, he'd earned himself a place on Team Two based out of Little Creek, Virginia. He served with distinction through multiple tours, climbing up the ranks and piling up the medals. And making the world a better, safer place in the best way he knew how.

His skillful and honorable service caught the US Special Operations Command's attention. Officers there selected Walker for inclusion in its top-level, top secret, experimental missions unit: Shadow Squadron.

As part of the elite unit of trainees, Walker worked with special operations personnel from every branch of the military. For several years now, he'd traveled throughout he world to perform top secret black ops

against nothing less than the forces of evil. He was probably too old to think of his job in such corny terms, but in his heart he still believed in the righteousness of the work he did. And he believed that if his friends and family back home knew about the work he did, they'd be proud of him.

If they saw him here and now, floating in these frigid, black waters, Walker wondered if his loved ones would be worried about him.

Walker was in the early stages of a mission, floating alongside the mighty leviathan *USS Georgia*. The vessel loomed in the water like one of the imaginary monsters of Walker's childhood. But here in the otherwise empty darkness, Walker found the sub's presence to be comforting, not frightening.

Sucking recycled air through his rebreather, Walker kick-stroked to the rear of the bullet-shaped Dry Deck Shelter near the *Georgia*. The DDS's circular rear hatch stood open. At the moment, four of his teammates were carefully sliding a black, torpedo-shaped vessel out into the ocean.

The vessel was a Swimmer Delivery Vehicle, though SEALs like Walker preferred to think of them as SEAL Delivery Vehicles. It served as an open submersible that could carry up to eight soldiers undetected. The SDV could travel distances greater than any person could reasonably be expected to swim, especially in frigid ocean waters. Walker had trained on SDVs for as long as he'd been a SEAL, and he and his fellow SDV soldiers secretly considered themselves to be a cut above even their "vanilla" SEAL brethren.

While Walker was no slouch at land navigation or airborne insertion, he was most at home in the water. He'd worked hard to see that every man on Shadow Squadron — especially those who'd come from the Army, Marines, and Air Force — completed their combat swimmer training with only the highest marks. He was still undoubtedly the best and most experienced combat swimmer on the unit, but he had total faith in his men's capabilities beneath the waves.

Of course, they weren't really his men, he had to admit. The JSOC had seen fit to recruit and saddle

him with a new commanding officer: Lieutenant Commander Daniel Cross.

It rankled Walker. Cross hadn't been in the Navy as long as he had. Cross hadn't been a SEAL as long as he had. Cross had combat experience, but not as much as Walker had. And worst of all, Cross wasn't even an SDV SEAL — he was pure "vanilla" SEAL. Before being recruited into Shadow Squadron, Cross had done more mountaineering and arctic survival training than SDV training.

So why did the JSOC put this man in charge of Shadow Squadron? Walker wondered.

On the positive side, Cross ran a clean op. Shadow Squadron hadn't lost a single man — so far. They'd faced pirates off the Somali coast, accomplishing their mission with slick professionalism and impressive flexibility. Walker worried, though, that their early successes were going to Cross's head.

Cross had come to Shadow Squadron with a reputation as a hero and a natural leader. In Walker's experience, that almost always went hand in hand with stubbornness and over-confidence. So far, the

lieutenant commander listened to input, and he suffered disagreement pretty well, but he was quick to halt discussion when he felt his point had been proven. True, Walker probably could argue with his CO a little less, but the man just seemed *too* smug. It was hard not to want to put him in his place once in a while.

But Commander Cross was right more often than he was wrong. That only made him all the more annoying.

Thankfully, Walker's sense of professionalism ensured that he put his feelings aside when the team was in the field. The men needed to see unity in their ranks. If he, the second-in-command, was always second-guessing and arguing with Cross, it would unsettle the others. A lack of focus would likely end up getting someone killed. So no matter what he thought of Cross personally, Walker knew he wouldn't be able to continue his service with another man's death on his conscience.

That didn't mean Walker had to keep his opinions to himself before Shadow Squadron's missions got underway, though . . .

* * *

Earlier that day, at dawn, Cross gathered his eight-man Shadow Squadron unit in the base ready room. The smell of fresh coffee hang thick in the air as all the other well-groomed men wearing camouflage fatigues shook off the morning weariness.

Cross, on the other hand, seemed to have plenty of energy. It was just one more reason for Walker to dislike him: Cross was a morning person.

"We've got a situation," Cross said energetically. He tapped on the computer-operated whiteboard on the wall and synced up with the room's tablet computer. "This one hits pretty close to home."

That got the men's attention. Ever since the events of 9/11, the fear of further terrorist action on American soil had loomed large over the nation. None were more sensitive to the terrorist threat than those in the military.

"I'm sure you're all familiar with the problems brewing in the waters just off Cuba," Cross said. He brought up a satellite map of the Gulf of Mexico, focusing on its eastern half.

Walker knew what Cross was referring to, but a quick glance at the other six men showed him that not everyone else understood.

The team's youngest member, the Air Force Combat Controller Staff Sergeant Edgar Brighton, raised his hand. "Sorry, Commander," he said, not looking sorry at all. "I get all my news from Jon Stewart and Stephen Colbert."

A few chuckles came from the other men. Walker glared at the young man, shaming Brighton and silencing the others. Brighton was a brave soldier and a technical genius, but he seemed to see himself as a class clown. Walker thought that was unbecoming conduct for an elite soldier.

"Sorry, Chief Walker," Brighton mumbled, having the decency to at least look embarrassed. He turned back to face Cross. "All the same, I'm still not quite sure what you're referring to, sir."

"It's all right," Cross said, taking it far too easy on Brighton for Walker's tastes. If Cross didn't make an example out of Brighton, the other men would start thinking it was okay to be so casual. Cross tapped

and swiped for a second on the tablet computer, bringing up an overlay on the whiteboard. Green and yellow zones showed up surrounding the coasts of the United States and Cuba. A blue zone appeared over the coast of Mexico. A roughly triangular gap appeared in the Gulf where the three zones didn't quite reach one another.

"For a few years now," Cross said, "the Chinese government has been negotiating with what's left of the Castro regime in Cuba for rights to drill for oil and natural gas in Cuba's territorial waters. Last month, Cuba agreed, and China set up its *Hēi Máo* gas and oil platform in the eastern Gulf of Mexico."

"*Hēi Máo* means *Black Anchor* in the Chinese language," Walker added.

Cross nodded, then tapped his tablet again. A red dot appeared in the northwestern part of the yellow zone with the words *Black Anchor* above it. Cross pointed at the red dot which was right next to the triangular gap. "It's Cuba's right to choose who they share their resources with, but their zone is right next to ours," he said. "For some folks in Congress, having

Hei Mao
Black Anchor

the Chinese float a GOPLAT in the Gulf at all makes them . . . uneasy."

That's an understatement, Walker thought. There was an awful lot of oil and natural gas buried beneath the Gulf of Mexico, but not every source was partitioned neatly. Quite often, more than one country had access to a reserve, causing tension between nations. Even worse, sometimes oil sources overlapped boundaries. That was a negotiations nightmare for all the countries involved.

"I can't say I'm thrilled about the situation either, Commander," Brighton said.

"Normally, this sort of thing is handled by the suits in Washington," Cross said, "But then yesterday, something happened." With another swipe across his tablet, the red dot on the whiteboard drifted northward. When the red dot crossed into the triangular region on the map, it vanished. "Yesterday the *Black Anchor* drifted into this doughnut hole here, then went dark."

A glance around gave Walker the impression that Cross's supposedly dramatic comment had just

left the men even more confused. Walker stood up, taking it upon himself to clarify the situation.

"The 'doughnut hole' is the spot between where the exclusive economic zones offshore of the United Stats, Mexico, and Cuba don't quite meet up together," Walker explained. "Arguing over ownership of the doughnut hole has been relatively quiet until China and Cuba started fighting over it recently."

"So how did this GOPLAT get installed there?" Brighton asked.

"It's not a fixed platform," Walker answered before Cross could. "It's a floating oil rig. It's supposed to be held in place by a set of anchors, but if the anchors are up, it can move around freely. That's part of the reason Congress put so much pressure on the President to raise a fuss when the Chinese put the *Black Anchor* where they did. They figured it was just a matter of time before the platform 'accidentally' ended up in the doughnut hole. Looks like Congress was right."

"Sounds like the President has a doughnut hole in his head," Brighton joked.

"That's your government you're talking about," Walker said sharply. "Show some respect."

"Sorry, Chief," Brighton said. He looked at Cross, as if seeking support. To his credit, Cross looked rather peeved at the young man, as well. Noting this, Brighton sat up straight. He added, "So when you say this thing went dark, Commander, I'm guessing it didn't really disappear."

"Nope," Cross said, changing the whiteboard display once more. It now showed an ocean-level view of the Chinese GOPLAT, as seen from several miles away. A set of map coordinates and a time stamp from the previous day appeared in the corner of the screen. The platform looked like an array of metal scaffoldings with a huge crane on top.

"We know exactly where it is — that isn't the problem," Cross said. "The *Black Anchor* radioed for resupply early last week, but since the resupply vessel came and went, all communication ceased."

"Do we know what happened?" Walker asked. He was still standing at the front of the ready room next to Cross even though he had nothing further to add.

"We didn't know until last night," Cross replied. "Shortly after the resupply vessel left, an unmarked speedboat showed up. It moored to the rig without permission and a team of armed men climbed aboard. They stormed the rig and took the crew hostage."

"Pirates again?" Brighton said. "I didn't even know the Gulf had pirates."

"They're not pirates," Cross said, his tone growing grim. "They're American mercenaries."

That statement blew away the last of the morning haze in the men. Their eyes grew wide and alert now.

Cross tapped his computer tablet once more, bringing up a file photo of a square-jawed blond man in his thirties. Below the picture was a corporate logo for some company called Hardwall Security.

"This is Corbin Van Sant," Cross said. "He and the attackers are private security contractors employed by Hardwall Security. The company's website claims they specialize in providing security at sea all around the world. Their 'onboard security experts' get paid to ride along with merchant vessels or escort ships to

protect clients from pirates and other criminals. They also occasionally patrol the coastlines at home for what they call 'unwelcome visitors.'"

"Like the vigilantes along the US-Mexico border," said Mark Shepherd.

"Except these guys are highly trained and efficient," Cross said.

"In other words, dangerous," said Walker.

Cross nodded. "They made headlines a few years ago for exposing a South American drug smuggling operation," he said. "But they spend most of their time searching for boats transporting illegal immigrants. The company's founder, Corbin Van Sant, has a reputation for a tough anti-immigration stance. He seems to think it's his personal mission to 'protect the sanctity of America's borders and waters.'"

"Sounds like a racist," one of the men mumbled. Walker saw it was Second Lieutenant Neil Larssen, one of the squadron's Rangers.

"So what happened, exactly?" Walker asked, redirecting the conversation. The more interruptions Cross allowed, the further off track this briefing would

get. "This Corbin Van Sant character just suddenly decided to go from American patriot to international pirate?"

"Specifics are sketchy," Cross said. "What we know so far is that Van Sant had one of his boats watching the *Black Anchor*. He sent it over the second the platform left Cuba's waters. His men probably tried to intimidate the Chinese into going back the way they came, and when the Chinese refused, things got out of hand. Now we have a hostage situation. We don't know any other details, though. For all I know, Van Sant's guys came to the platform with every intention of hijacking it."

"How do we know this much in the first place, sir?" asked Lieutenant Kimiyo Yamashita, the team's sniper. The stoic Army Ranger rarely spoke during mission briefings, which Walker appreciated, but something about this mission had apparently piqued his curiosity. "Have the Cubans asked us for help resolving it? Or the Chinese?"

"No," Cross admitted. "The Chinese argue that the doughnut hole in the Gulf is in international

waters. They believe they're within their rights. We only learned what we know from —"

"Spying?" Yamashita interrupted. He said it in a flat tone, without judgment.

"Yep," Cross confirmed matter-of-factly. "Now, obviously, American citizens taking Chinese and Cuban nationals hostage is a big problem. Everybody's trying to keep it out of the news for now, but there's only so long that's going to be in the victims' best interests. When the press gets wind of this, the United States is going to end up looking bad. The Chinese and Cubans are trying to negotiate with Van Sant's people, but we believe they're just stalling until they can mount a rescue operation. When they do, we'll be facing a major international incident."

"Not that we aren't already," Walker put in.

"Which is where we come in," Cross said. "We're going to board the *Black Anchor* before anyone else can, free those prisoners, and deal with the Hardwall mercs who took them hostage."

"Deal with them?" Brighton asked. "You mean like . . ." He pointed his finger to his temple.

"I'm hoping it doesn't come to that," Cross said.

"With all due respect," Walker said, "these are American citizens we're talking about."

"They are criminals," Cross said.

"American criminals, sir," Walker added. "We should take every effort to capture them alive so they can stand trial."

"These men are terrorizing foreign nationals in the name of one man's political agenda," Cross said. "They're an embarrassment to what our country stands for. If they force our hand, I will not make it easy for them."

"All the same —" Walker began.

"This isn't a discussion, Chief," Cross said sternly. "Now sit down. We have some work to do."

* * *

Walker's pride still stung as they traveled in the SDV. He wasn't normally the type to sulk, and was disappointed in himself for not just shrugging it off and carrying on as normal.

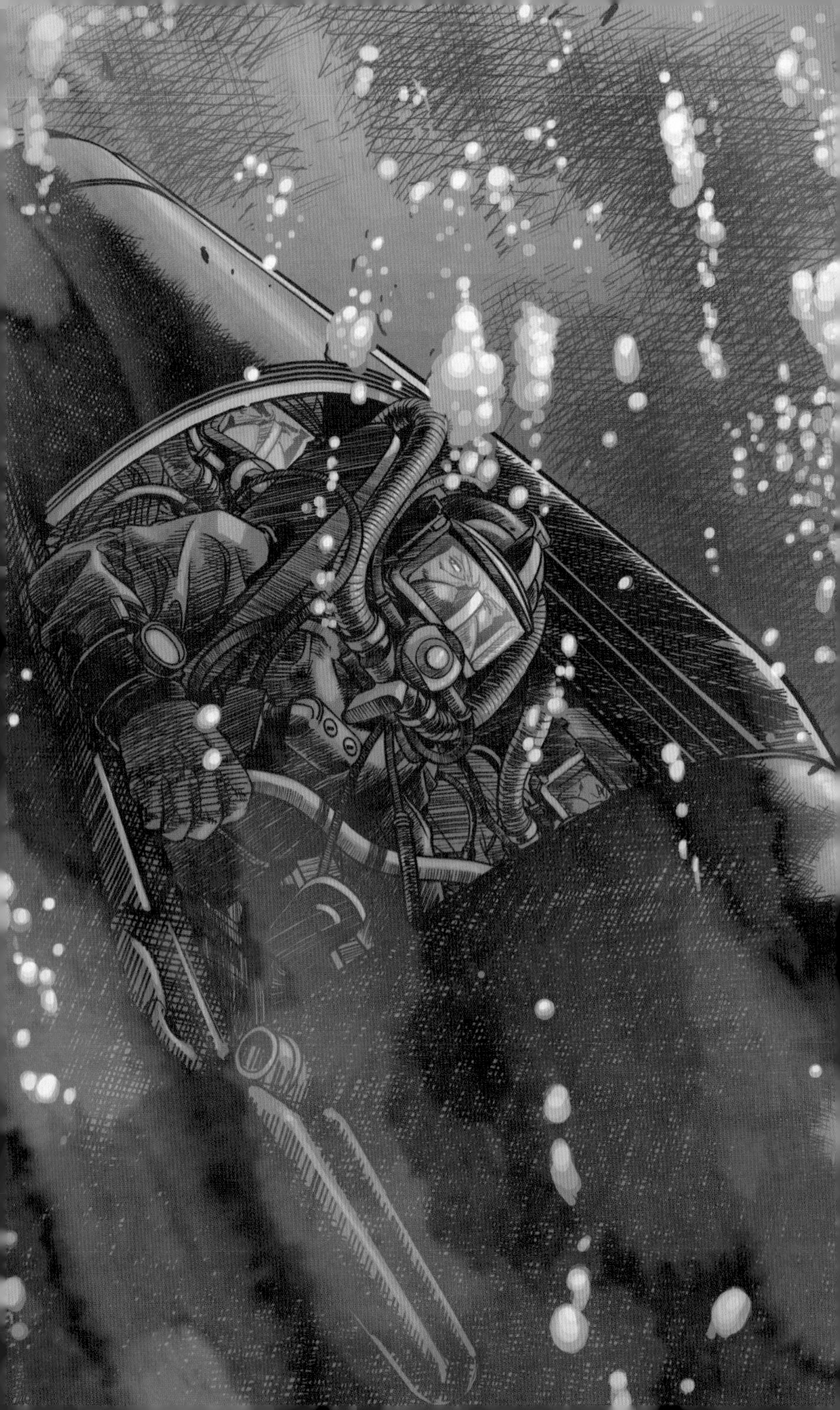

But now wasn't the time to feel sorry for himself. From here on out, floating in the moonlit waters, the team was on noise discipline until the hostages and mercenaries were seen to. After that, Walker would figure out a way to tell his senior officer what he really thought of him.

But that just made the long, silent trip toward the *Black Anchor* feel even longer.

5514.108

INTEL

DECRYPTING

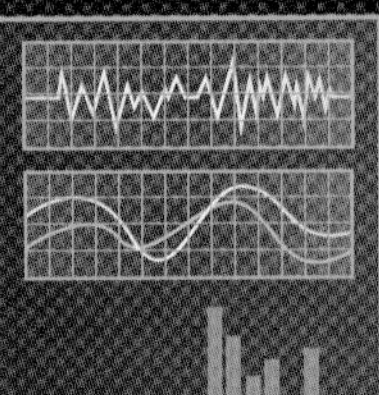

12345

COM CHATTER

- M4 CARBINE – short and light selective-fire assault rifle
- MERCENARY – paid-for-hire soldier
- SONAR – method of identifying objects underwater that uses echolocation
- SUPPRESSOR – device attached to a firearm that reduces the amount of noise and muzzle flash when fired

3245.98

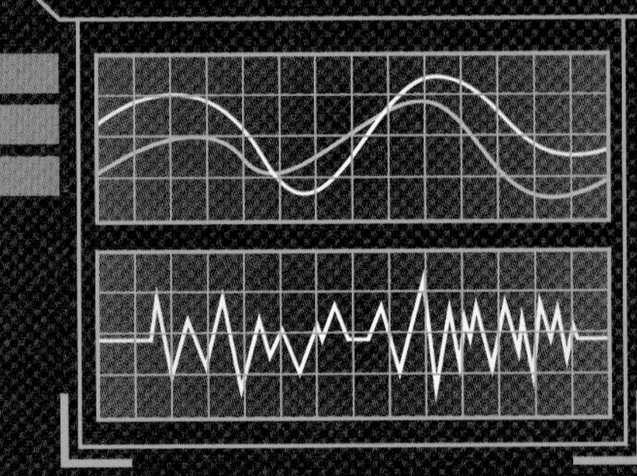

CHAPTER TWO

1324.014

INFILTRATION

Deep under the surface, the SDV glided through the water carrying its six combat swimmers. Chief Walker piloted the vehicle while Cross sat beside him, navigating by GPS and SONAR. The instruments gave off the only visible light.

In the rear compartment sat Staff Sergeant Brighton, Second Lieutenant Larssen, Lieutenant Yamashita, and Hospital Corpsman Second Class Kyle Williams. All six men sat in nearly total darkness, breathing on regulators attached to the SDV's onboard air tanks.

An SDV insertion wasn't ideal for an assault on a gas-and-oil platform. Fast-roping down from a

hovering helicopter would have suited better. But stealth was a much higher priority this time out than speed.

It wasn't so much the hostiles the team had to worry about as much as the Cuban patrol boats around the *Black Anchor*. If one of those crafts spotted them sneaking in, they might assume the wrong thing — that the US government was trying to sneak out the Hardwall mercenaries. That would almost certainly lead to hostility.

So the team chose the SDV approach, which filled Chief Walker with quiet satisfaction. Cross had initially argued for a fast-rope in, then for the Zodiac, almost as if he were afraid of using an SDV.

Patiently, and with respect, Walker had poked holes in each of Cross's suggestions for insertion until the SDV was the only option left. To be fair, Cross was qualified for SDV operations and he was a skilled navigator. However, Walker couldn't help but assume the lieutenant commander beside him was squirming with discomfort the whole time. And considering how far away in US waters they'd had to

launch the SDV to avoid detection, it was an awful long time indeed.

Eventually, the *Black Anchor* platform showed up on the instruments. Walker maneuvered over to it. With practicied precision, he brought the SDV alongside the submerged structure. Then he cut the engines.

Walker nodded to Cross. Cross killed the instrumentation lights and hit the release to open the doors. The pair of them switched from the SDV's air supply to their own rebreathers. Then, still deep beneath the surface of the water, they exited the vehicle together.

Behind them, Brighton, Larssen, Yamashita, and Williams emerged. While Cross moored the SDV to the *Black Anchor*, the others glided over to the side of the spar and gently kick-stroked upward alongside it, taking great care to ascend slowly and silently.

Large blue and white LEDs dotted the outside of the tubes. They provided just enough illumination in the nighttime sea to lend the entire platform an alien appearance. Staring up at the overwhelming

size of the rig, Walker could find no better word for it than *amazing.*

The underside of the *Black Anchor* consisted of six sealed vertical tubes wound around a seventh center tube. The tubes were hollow and allowed the rig to float or sink, depending on when the crew flushed or filled them with sea water.

Walker glanced at the set of four thick anchor chains that extended out into the darkness. It appeared that the crew had not been given a chance to extend the platform's drilling apparatus before the Hardwall mercenaries arrived.

Lieutenant Commander Cross quickly secured the SDV and signaled to Walker that it was time to go.

The pair of them followed the other four men up. They rose together at a leisurely pace so they didn't decompress too quickly. If they didn't pace themselves, then nitrogen bubbles would expand rapidly in their bloodstream, giving them decompression sickness. That would bring a quick end to the mission — and probably their lives.

Fortunately, the sea was relatively calm, so they didn't have to fight strong currents to stay on course.

As they neared the surface, they found steel emergency ladders running up the outside of the tubes. Cross took the lead, swimming over to the nearest ladder. He ascended to just below the surface of the water, then stopped to look back at his men. They spread out below Cross so they could all see him. Walker could practically feel their excitement electrifying the water around them.

Cross's first signal was for total noise discipline. It was pointless underwater, but vital topside. If they lost the element of surprise against the mercenary hostiles, the hostages would likely be the ones to suffer for it.

Next Cross set the climbing order. He would go first, followed by Walker, Brighton, Yamashita, then Williams. Larssen would take the rear.

When the swimmers finished shuffling their positions in the water, Cross held up one hand as if he were holding an invisible tennis ball. It wasn't a standard military hand signal, but a reminder of

a certain point Cross had relentlessly driven into their heads throughout training: *think spherically.*

It was a vital concept, especially on a structure like this. Incoming attacks wouldn't be restricted to just the front and rear as on a normal battlefield. On this rig, with so many levels, enemies could just as easily attack from above or below, so the men had to be ready for trouble to come at them from every direction. Spherically.

Cross had repeated the concept constantly in training, making the hand signal every single time. *Think spherically, think spherically, think spherically.* It was solid advice, even if the repetition had gotten on Walker's nerves long ago.

Finally, Cross nodded to his men, looped an elbow around the ladder, and begin to remove his diving fins. The other five soldiers got in order below and did likewise, tucking the fins behind their backs under the straps holding on their small complement of gear. When his booted feet were free, Cross began the long climb upward. The squad followed.

When Walker broke the surface, his sense of weight suddenly returned, as if he were an astronaut coming back from a long journey in space. Now he felt every pound of his gear, though he tried not to let it slow him down. A stiff breeze chilled the water on his hands and face, and the gentle muffling of sound beneath the waves was replaced by the harsh splash and crash of the waves below.

Under the full moon's light, Walker could now see much farther. The improved view showed him the Cuban patrol boats waiting in the distance for their chance to close in and turn this mission into a total mess.

Cuba's naval fleet wasn't all that impressive compared to America's modern ships, but could still do plenty of damage. Intel told them that at least one Chinese vessel was nearby as well, though Walker couldn't see well enough to pick it out. But he did identify the mercenaries' boat moored on the other side of the platform.

If things went according to plan, it wouldn't matter how many boats were out on the water, or

where they were located. But Walker knew that few plans remained intact after first contact with the enemy. Adaptation was almost a certainty in missions. Van Sant's men could certainly testify to that — that is, if they hadn't come planning to take hostages in the first place.

After a short climb, Cross reached the top of the ladder, coming to the underside of a metal catwalk. He suddenly gave the stop signal, and Walker passed it down even though he wasn't sure what the holdup was. He got his answer a moment later. A mercenary strolled by on a long, lonely patrol of the catwalk.

This particular metal walkway was the lowest level on the platform that was still above water. The single sentry had likely been stationed down here to watch for boats trying to sneak people on board.

Walker smiled. Cross had to realize that if he'd had his way and inserted via Zodiac instead of SDV, this sentry would have seen them and raised the alarm. Or worse, the mercs would have waited until they boarded and then cut them down on the ladder as they climbed up.

But because they'd done things Walker's way instead of Cross's, the team had remained undetected. They also gained the safety of the shadows beneath the walkway.

The sentry wore black fatigues, combat boots, and a Bluetooth earpiece. Slung around his shoulder was a Heckler & Koch MP5A3 submachine gun. A ballistic vest covered his broad chest. As he paced, his eyes remained focused on the thrashing waters below, hoping to spot and prevent any attempted insertions — like the one Shadow Squadron had just successfully performed.

The sentry continued his circuit, passing by the ladder where Cross's team waited below. He was entirely unaware of their presence. As the sentry passed, Cross signaled to Walker.

Quietly, Cross snuck up behind the mercenary with Walker on his heels. As soon as they reached the walkway, Cross rushed up behind the guard and slapped a choke hold around his neck. Cross's muscles tightened. He squeezed the man's windpipe and pulsing arteries closed.

Cross pulled the sentry to his knees, his weight pulling the man backward. The mercenary tried to reach for his submachine gun hanging around his shoulder.

SLIT!

Walker cut the gun strap using his knife, and took the weapon from the merc. He casually pitched it over the side of the safety rail and into the ocean.

Unable to shout for help, and growing weaker from the lack of blood flow to his brain, the sentry flailed wildly. He clawed at Cross's forearm. Cross took the blows, patiently waiting for the sentry to slip into unconsciousness.

The mercenary went for his boot knife, but Walker snatched the weapon away before he could reach it. Finally, the merc's eyes slowly slipped shut and he slumped into Cross's arms.

Cross carefully laid him on the catwalk. He checked his pulse, then nodded. With Walker's help, Cross flipped the merc over onto his belly.

Walker kept a lookout while Cross produced a pair of plastic zip ties from his pocket.

ZIP!

ZIP!

Walker secured the man's hands behind his back. After that, he secured one ankle to the metal walkway rail. A quick search revealed the man had no other weapons or ID of any sort.

Walker pitched the man's knife into the churning waters below, then did the same with the man's Bluetooth headset. Only then did he signal for the rest of the team to come up the ladder to the walkway.

Brighton, Yamashita, Williams, and Larssen took their positions. Williams checked the downed mercenary. He was alive but deeply unconscious. Willaims nodded once to Cross.

The six of them then spent a moment pocketing their swimming gear and readying their weapons. Each of them was armed with a suppressor-equipped

M4 carbine with a modified, shorter barrel for the inevitable close-quarters combat that this mission would require.

Staff Sergeant Brighton had complained about that during the mission briefing, clearly hoping to use his prized AA-12 combat shotgun aboard the *Black Anchor*. However, Cross had accurately pointed out that the AA-12 just put too much lead into the air for this mission. And it was anything but precise — even if Brighton argued otherwise. Which he had. Repeatedly.

When everyone was ready, Cross gathered the squad and addressed them once more without words. He held up five fingers, reminding them of the number of hostile targets remaining onboard.

The Cubans' intelligence suggested that only six Hardwall mercenaries had gotten off their boat and subdued the oil platform's crew. Presumably, all five of the remaining mercs were armed and armored similarly to the sentry they'd just incapacicated. And they were sure to be in contact with each other via their headsets.

Cross tapped his watch, indicating it was only a matter of time before the other mercs noticed the missing man was no longer keeping in contact.

That meant Shadow Squadron would have to move fast. And quietly.

According to the Cubans' intelligence, the Hardwall men were keeping the hostages near the helipad.

Cross circled one finger in the air, mimicking a helicopter's spinning propeller. The message was clear: reaching the helipad was their first priority.

Walker knew this without having to read hand signals. Freeing the hostages was the utmost of importance on any mission. Engaging hostiles before securing the hostages almost always led to the loss of life.

Finally, Cross held up the *think spherically* signal one more time. As one, the men each gave a sharp nod.

Together, they moved out along the catwalk to a set of stairs farther on. Their eyes — and the

muzzles of their carbines — kept in constant motion, scanning for trouble from all directions. Up, down, left, right — the enemies could come from anywhere here.

It didn't take Shadow Squadron long to find the trouble they went looking for.

5514.108

INTEL

DECRYPTING

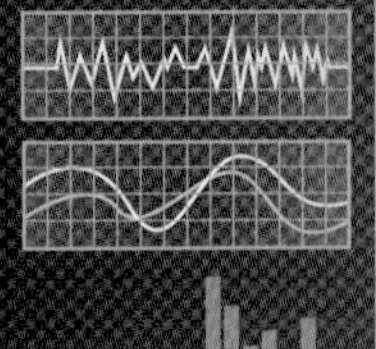

12345

COM CHATTER

- BALLISTIC VEST – bulletproof piece of armor worn across the torso
- CANALPHONE – headphones that fit inside the canal of the ear
- MP5 – German-made, 9mm submachine gun
- SEAHAWK – helicopter designed specifically for traveling over water

3245.98

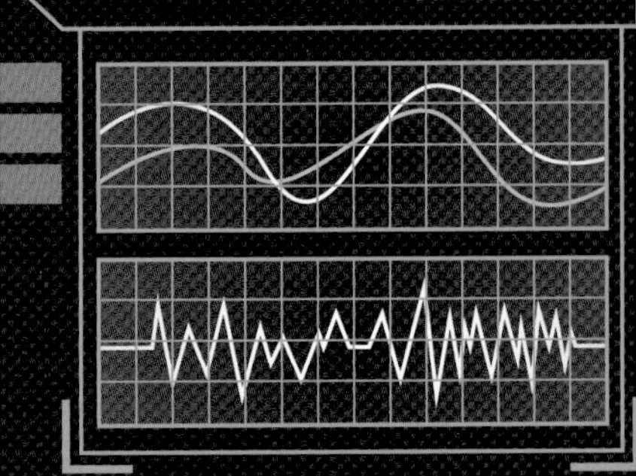

CHAPTER THREE

1324.014

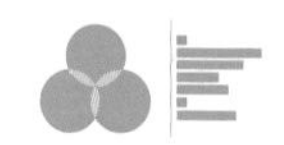

ASSAULT

The stairs up from the lower catwalk led up to the center of the structure where they found a nexus of stairways, ladders, and walkways. It resembled a spider's nest made of metal. An array of dim LEDs created a creepy web of intersecting shadows and dark spaces where enemies could hide.

Walker strained his ears listening for any sound of approaching mercenaries. He peered around, finding the stairs and walkways all labeled in Chinese. That wasn't a problem for him, since he was fluent, but he saw confusion on his teammates' faces.

Walker pointed out two separate paths that would take the team to the helipad. Cross gave a quick

grateful nod and split the cell into two fireteams. He took Yamashita and Williams in one direction and Walker led Brighton and Larssen in the other. Walker's men crossed the underside of the helipad to a metal ladder on the far side. The three of them climbed until Walker reached the top and stopped. Carefully, he peered over the edge to take stock of the situation.

Twenty or so miserable-looking Chinese and Cuban hostages sat huddled in the center of the helipad. They were leaning against each other for warmth, or shivering with their arms wrapped around themselves. None of them spoke to each other or to their captors. To Walker's eyes, none of them appeared to be injured or otherwise suffering, but it would be Williams's job to say for sure.

Walker scanned for mercenaries. Two of them had been left to guard the hostages. Like the man down on the catwalk, the guards wore ballistic vests and carried submachine guns. One of them stood at the edge of the helipad looking out over the ocean, holding a writhing, pitiful Chinese crewman by his neck. The other guard stood by the group of hostages

in the center. The second guard was laughing as the hostage in the mercenary's grasp squirmed.

"What's the matter?" the mercenary demanded of his terrified prisoner. "Don't have to use the bathroom anymore? Don't be shy, we're all guys here. Go ahead, do your business."

Walker clenched his teeth. He had to struggle to repress the urge to aim his M4 one-handed and drop the thug where he stood. Yet, as satisfying as that might be, he couldn't be sure that the man wouldn't knock the prisoner overboard. And Walker didn't want to get into the habit of shooting people just because they were bullies.

CLICK-A-CLICK. The waterproof canalphone in Walker's right ear activated. Walker scanned across the helipad for Lieutenant Commander Cross's fireteam. He could just make out Cross crouching at the top of the stairway leading onto the helipad on the other side of the platform.

Walker tapped his canalphone twice, returning Cross's signal. Cross took aim at the mercenary closest to himself who was standing near the bulk of the

hostages. Walker tensed on the ladder, preparing to move on the hostile who was harassing the captured crewman. He glanced back at Brighton, and held up three fingers. Then two. Then one . . .

The men launched into action, performing a variation on a set of maneuvers they had practiced many times in training. Cross stood up into full view of both guards and actually whistled to get their attention. It was just the kind of grandstanding that Walker found most annoying about Cross. However, it was undeniably effective: both guards turned to look at Cross in stunned surprise. That was when Walker mounted the helipad deck from the ladder.

Cross fired a single round.

BANG!

The guard folded up in the middle and sank to his knees. The hostages scrambled back away from him, parting for Cross as he rushed over to the downed mercenary.

A moment after Cross fired, the Hardwall mercenary by the edge of the helipad reacted with predictable cowardice. He yanked his gasping Chinese prisoner around in a half circle and clutched him from behind as a human shield. The mercenary brought his submachine gun up one-handed over the hostage's shoulder and pointed it at Cross.

Walker momentarily considered blasting the submachine gun out of the mercenary's hand. Instead, he aimed down at the mercenary's right thigh.

POP!

The bullet drilled right through his leg. The mercenary yelped and collapsed as his leg buckled, giving his human shield a chance to dash over to his huddled coworkers.

That's good at least, Walker reflected. However, the wounded mercenary was aware of him now, and he was still perfectly capable of firing his weapon. As the merc flopped onto his back, he started to raise his gun with one hand.

"Drop it!" Walker demanded, reluctant to shoot an American citizen. "Now!"

Whether the man would have complied or not, Walker would never know. No sooner had Walker shouted his warning when Lieutenant Commander Cross raised his M4 and put the issue to rest, squeezing off a shot that caught the mercenary's MP5 right above the trigger.

KARRRANG!

Hot metal shrapnel burst from the weapon as it flew out of the man's hand. When the ruined submachine gun clattered to the deck, Cross shot it again.

KACHUNK!

The weapon skittered over the side of the helipad and into the ocean.

Walker glanced at Cross, glaring at the man who'd potentially just saved his life. Cross flicked Walker a salute and a smirk. Walker just shook his head and turned away. He wasn't going to begrudge Cross for taking the shot, but did the man have to show off when he did it?

Brighton and Larssen had climbed up onto the helipad behind Walker. They moved past him to zip-cuff the wounded mercenary. They pulled off his Bluetooth headset, bound his hands behind his back, and then treated his nonfatal leg wound. Walker let the man lie and joined Cross. The lieutenant commander was just finishing zip-cuffing the other mercenary. The Hardwall man lay on his stomach gasping for air, trying to recover from being struck by Cross's first shot. The bullet had been stopped by the ballistic vest, sparing his life, but knocking the wind out of him.

The stunned hostages milled around, staring at the American soldiers with every imaginable variety of dumbfounded shock. Two bullets, two

incapacitated guards, no deaths. Walker had to admit that Cross did well. Really well.

Cross looked over at Walker and mouthed the word, "Clear?" Walker nodded. Williams came over at the same time, leaving Yamashita to keep a lookout for the rest of the hostiles. For the moment, none of the three remaining Hardwall mercs were anywhere to be seen. So Williams walked among the skittish hostages, looking for obvious signs of trauma and asking quiet questions.

Walker approached the hostage whom the second mercenary had tried to use as a human shield. "Are you hurt?" he whispered in Chinese.

The hostage's glassy, confused eyes slowly came back into focus. He shook his head. "They didn't hurt us," the man said in a soft, breathless voice.

"Do you know how many guards are left?" Walker asked.

"Four," the hostage answered. "One is on the catwalk below."

Walker nodded. That one was no longer a problem. "Where are the rest?" he asked.

"Operations control, with the station chief," the hostage said, pointing up toward the highest point of the facility. "They're talking to my government."

Walker relayed that information to Cross. The lieutenant commander stood as Brighton and Larssen dragged the wounded mercenary over to them. The hostages backed off again. The mercenary moaned and tried to clutch at his leg with his zip-cuffed hands, cursing and yelling at them.

"Can we give this guy something to shut him up?" Brighton whispered in annoyance to Cross and Williams. "He's going to give our position away."

"I've got something for him," Cross said, stepping next to the wounded man. The mercenary looked up as he Cross slammed the butt of his carbine square into the merc's forehead. The man fell flat on his back, and his head bounced off the deck. He lost consciousness instantly.

"Oh!" Brighton said, flinching and hiding his mouth behind his hand. Then, with a huge grin, he crouched over the unconscious mercenary. "You all right, man?" Brighton joked. "Walk it off, buddy."

"Shh!" Walker hissed, giving Brighton the noise-discipline signal. The combat controller snapped back to his feet, his face turning red.

"All right, form up," Cross said softly, calling his men together. "We've got three hostiles remaining. They are in or around the op center at the top of the facility." He addressed Williams. "Stay and give the hostages a once-over." Then he looked at Larssen. "Watch his back, and keep an eye on the injured mercenaries."

"Sir," Williams and Larssen said together.

"You three are with me," Cross said to Walker, Yamashita, and Brighton. "Let's go sew this one up."

"Sir," Yamashita and Brighton said. Walker only gave a curt nod.

The fireteam joined the lieutenant commander and left the helipad. With eyes and gun barrels sweeping back and forth and up and down, the men moved up a metal stairway to the platform's upper levels. The stairway wrapped around the outside of the platform and led into a narrow exterior walkway with pipes, valves, and gauges on both sides.

From there, the team passed through a wire-strewn computer center, a sparse recreation room with a television and ping-pong table, and the kitchen and dining area. Each room was messy and cluttered, evidence suggesting that the Hardwall men had rousted the crew in the middle of the workday. But there was no sign of more hostiles.

After clearing the rooms on that level, the team emerged onto another walkway. It wrapped around the other side of the structure, leading to another stairway to the topmost levels. Before the fireteam reached the stairs, Cross suddenly gave the stop signal. He looked over the rail at the helipad below. Walker looked down as well, trying to figure out what had caught the lieutenant commander's attention.

Walker saw that the hostages had grouped up at the edge of the helipad closest to the center of the platform. Williams moved among them, making sure everyone was in good health. Larssen was finishing zip-cuffing the two mercenaries to a stair railing. Faint smears of blood shone in the lights, indicating where Larssen had dragged the unconscious, wounded mercenary over to the rail.

"Lieutenants," Cross breathed, tapping his canalphone. "Did either of you call for medical evac?"

"Negative," Larssen and Williams both answered, confusion evident in their voices.

Walker shared their confusion for a moment until he heard what Cross had already noticed: the sound of helicopter blades chopping through the night air. The Navy had a Seahawk chopper on standby in case of emergencies. But this incoming helicopter didn't sound like a Seahawk, and it wasn't coming from the right direction.

All too quickly, the aircraft roared up out of the darkness. It threw blinding halogen spotlights onto the helipad. One light played over the frightened hostages. The other spotlight illuminated Larssen, who was just crossing the helipad to rejoin Williams.

Cross and Walker both recognized the make of the helicopter as it rose into view. It was a Russian-made Mil Mi-8 — a troop transport and fast-attack gunship employed by both the Chinese and the Cuban militaries. The hostages' countrymen had

come to rescue them at last. And now, in a huddled mass of terrified hostages, they had spotted an armed soldier standing over them.

The chopper turned its broadside toward the landing pad. A door in the side slid open. "Get out of there!" Walker and Cross called, hitting their canalphones simultaneously. Their warning was too late.

RAT-A-TAT-TAT-TAT-TAT-TAT-TAT-TAT!

RAT-A-TAT-TAT-TAT-TAT-TAT-TAT-TAT!

Machine guns flared to life as bullets drew a crisscrossing line across the concrete right toward Larssen. He had already started running away from the hostages and toward cover, but he wasn't fast enough. Larssen's body jerked, spun, and fell — all in the blink of an eye. He landed only a few yards short of safety. The helicopter lowered toward the pad, preparing to offload soldiers.

Cross pointed toward the helicopter. "Yamashita," he said through clenched teeth. "Tail rotor."

"Sir," Yamashita said without a hint of emotion in his voice.

As one, Yamashita and Cross raised their weapons and fired in the helicopter's direction.

POP!

POP!

POP!

Walker had to admit his commanding officer was one of the best shots he had ever seen. The lieutenant commander managed to squeeze off two three-round

bursts that dug into the helicopter's hull just below were the spinning main rotor. A third burst followed, raising a thick plume of white smoke.

SKREEEEEEEEEEEEEE!

The helicopter's engine squealed like a wounded animal.

As good a shot as Cross was, however, Yamashita was even better. Firing one bullet at a time, he punched a line of holes in the helicopter's narrow tail, damaging the mechanism of the stabilizing rotor on the rear.

The chopper bucked suddenly in the air. It swerved wildly to one side. The pilot fought the spin and just barely managed to keep it from slamming into the edge of the helipad and crashing into the ocean below.

Walker saw the gunmen inside clinging to the handholds for dear life. They were unable to even find where the shots were coming from, much less return fire.

"Cease fire," Cross ordered. He and Yamashita lowered their weapons.

Barely able to control the aircraft, the pilot veered away from the *Black Anchor* and raced back the way he'd come. The helicopter fishtailed across the sky like a car swerving on an icy road.

Walker assumed the craft had launched from one of the vessels keeping watch on the water. He wondered if it would be able to make it back and land in one piece.

"Williams!" Cross barked, pointing over the rail toward where Larssen lay bleeding. It was technically a breach of operational protocol to refer to any of the team members by name while engaged in the field, but Walker could hardly fault the slip.

"Got him," came Williams's response over the canalphone. The corpsman rushed across the helipad and crouched over Larssen. He broke out the first-aid kit he hadn't yet needed for the hostages. A moment later, Williams said, "He's alive, Commander — barely. We need our evac chopper."

Cross had already produced a waterproof radio

from one of his cargo pockets. He keyed in the emergency frequency. "Angel, this is Preacher," he called, concealing the distress in his voice. "Man down. We need an airlift."

"Preacher, this is Angel," the pilot of the standby chopper called back. "Roger that, Preacher. ETA is five minutes."

Cross signed off. Then he tapped his canalphone and said, "Five minutes, Williams."

Williams sighed. "Sir."

"I'll gather our dive gear," Brighton said, turning as if to head back down below.

"Leave it," Cross said, stowing the radio. "You heard the man, we've only got five minutes."

"Sir?" Brighton said.

"Three hostiles left," Cross said, "and one hostage."

The distress from seeing Larssen down, and possibly dying, was absent from Cross's face now. In its place was a cold, grim anger. "Let's move," he barked.

"What about the SDV?" Brighton asked.

"The Navy can send a SEAL team if they want it back," Cross replied. "Now move out."

Brighton opened his mouth to say something else, but was silenced by the chattering of submachine gun fire.

5514.108

INTEL

DECRYPTING

12345

COM CHATTER

- CROSSFIRE – lines of fire that overlap each other
- FIRETEAM – a small unit of soldiers
- M84 FLASHBANG – a nonlethal grenade that temporarily deafens and blinds those caught in its blast
- SUPPRESSING FIRE – gunfire used to render a target temporarily ineffective or unusable

3245.98

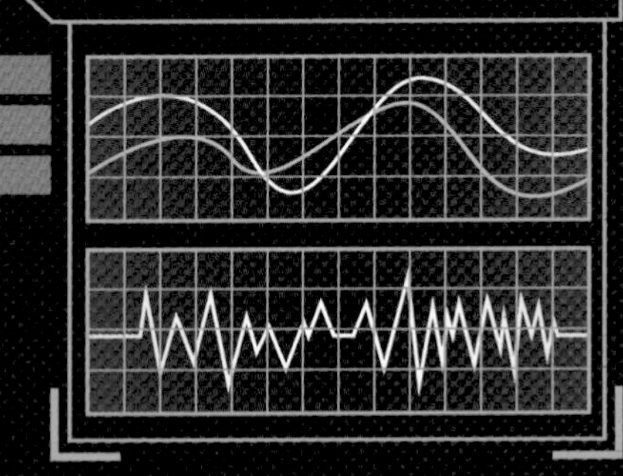

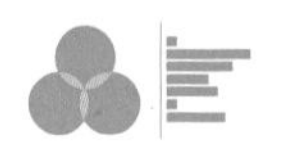

CHAPTER FOUR

FIREFIGHT

Bullets roared from ahead and above, ringing off the walls, and the metal catwalk. Walker saw where the shots came from and realized what must have happened. The hostiles, unaware of Shadow Squadron's arrival, had heard the chopper open fire. The sudden departure of the helicopter had undoubtedly surprised them, but now they'd spotted Cross's fireteam, realizing they were still under siege. Fortunately, rather than move in for the kill or spread out to coordinate a crossfire, they'd simply opened fire from where they stood.

Two mercenaries were shooting from the catwalk one level up. Most of their shots were wild and

panicked, though one glanced off Cross's helmet and another grazed Brighton across the shoulder blade.

The fireteam immediately took cover. Walker had the clearest line of sight on the gunmen. He threw a line of fire up toward them, sending them diving backward for cover.

Cross angrily signaled the team to move up and take the stairway, unwilling to let up on the mercenaries now that they'd engaged. Walker laid down cover fire to keep the mercenaries' heads down.

RAT-A-TAT-TAT!

Hissing in pain from the wound on his back, Brighton rushed to a position at the foot of the steps and fired a few rounds up over the men's heads. Yamashita backtracked and scrambled up a ladder, looking for a level field of fire. One of the mercenaries saw him climbing and fired off what was left in his clip, but Walker drove him back with another stream of suppressing fire. The other mercenary fired back, forcing Yamashita to roll around a corner, and kept his head down.

For a moment, no one moved and no one fired. The Hardwall men couldn't come down, and Yamashita had a firing line on their only avenue of escape. However, the mercs had clear lanes of fire on the only route the fireteam could take to reach them.

They were at a stalemate. Time was running out.

Suddenly, Lieutenant Commander Cross stood up. With his back to a wall, he moved toward a position directly beneath where the two mercenaries were holed up together. Then he signaled Walker to join Brighton at the base of the stairs and for the two of them to get ready to move.

Walker frowned. Yamashita wasn't in a position to provide covering fire. He only had a line on the mercenaries' escape route. If Brighton and Walker went up the stairs, the mercenaries would have a nice, narrow lane of fire to cut them down.

What is Cross thinking? Walker wondered.

Reading the expression on Walker's face, Cross winked, then gave him the think spherically sign. He reached into his belt and drew an M84 flashbang grenade, then nodded at the walkway overhead.

Walker still wasn't sure exactly what Cross had in mind, but he got ready to move just the same. Cross pulled the pin, but held the spoon and started counting down from five on his free hand. At two, he let go of the spoon but held onto the grenade, letting its fuse cook off in his hand. At zero, he signaled for Walker and Brighton to go, and the two men immediately rushed up the stairs together, staring down the long stretch of walkway between themselves and the mercs.

Hearing their approach, the mercs leaned around with their weapons. At the same moment, Cross took one step out from under the catwalk and threw his flashbang straight up in the air. It popped up over the rail right next to the mercenaries' boots.

POP!

The flare and the concussion knocked the mercs off their feet, giving Walker and Brighton all the time they needed to close in and disarm them.

Cross and Yamashita quickly joined them. Walker signaled for Brighton to keep an eye out for the last mercenary. Then Walker went to work zip-cuffing the mercenaries to the catwalk.

With that done, Walker pulled out both men's Bluetooth headsets and put one to his left ear. Cross took the other one and did the same, signaling his fireteam to advance on the op center.

"What the heck is going on out there?!" the last remaining mercenary shouted through the earpiece. "Somebody answer me!"

"It's over," Cross said. "The rest of your men have been neutralized."

There was a long pause. Then a voice asked, "Who is this?"

To Walker, the mercenary sounded scared and angry — a dangerous combination.

"Give yourself up," Cross responded. "You've run out of time, and I lack patience to argue with you."

The mercenary let out a half-crazed cackle. "Oh, really?" he said. "Does that mean I should just kill my hostage, then?"

Cross frowned. Walker wondered if the lieutenant commander had forgotten there was one hostage left.

The fireteam made it to the last walkway that led to the operations command station. The station had a large window on the side, but the lights inside went out as the team approached. Cross signaled a halt in front of the one door that led inside.

"No answer to that, huh?" the mercenary said. Walker could hear a second person whimpering in the background whenever the man talked. Walker glanced at Cross, but the commander remained silent.

"I'll tell you what," the merc said. "Me and my new friend here are going to get on my boat and leave, and you're going to let us. If anybody tries to 'neutralize' me, I swear —"

"Forget it," Cross snapped.

"No?" the merc said. "Then come in here and get me. The second I hear running footsteps, I'm putting two bullets in the back of this guy's head and coming out with guns blazing."

Cross clenched his teeth. Then he closed his eyes and took a deep breath. He seemed to be considering daring the mercenary to do just that.

"Wait," Walker said, addressing both the mercenary and Cross. Walker held up a hand, silently urging Cross to give him a moment. Cross reluctantly nodded.

"Who's this now?" the mercenary demanded.

"Let me explain the situation to you," Walker said, his voice steady, and heavy with authority. "In two minutes, a helicopter's coming to pick us up. And we're all going to be on it because you can be sure that the Cubans are already on their way here to clean up this mess their own way."

"Wait," the mercenary said, his voice sounding rattled all of a sudden. "Who are you guys? Are you Americans? Did Van Sant send you?"

"You're running out of time," Walker said. "If you don't come out, we're just going to leave and let you have this conversation with the Cubans. And I promise you, if you kill that hostage, you're on your own."

"Hang on a second, I —" the merc began.

"It's now or never," Walker said, interrupting him. Walker held up the earpiece so the merc could hear the approaching chopper. "Our ride's here. What's it going to be?"

At first, nothing happened. Then, slowly, the mercenary opened the op center door and stepped out. He froze when he saw four M4 barrels pointing at him down the walkway.

"All right," he started to say. "Let's just —"

"Put your weapon down," Walker ordered him.

KLANK-KLANK!

The mercenary dropped his MP5 on the ground and put his hands up, uncertainty on his face. Cross dropped the Bluetooth headset and crunched it underfoot. He walked over to the mercenary.

"Kick the weapon over here," Walker said, coming up behind Cross. The mercenary slid the gun across the floor. Cross stepped over it, letting Walker catch it under one foot. "Now get —"

Williams's voice cut in on the team's canalphones. "Commander," the corpsman said, his voice somber. "Neil's . . . not going to make it."

Cross's face went dark. "What?" the mercenary asked, unable to hear the conversation but reacting to the sudden change in Cross's expression. "What's going on?"

Cross brought up his M4 and smashed the butt stock across the bridge of the mercenary's nose.

KRUNCH!!

The mercenary stumbled backward, bounced off the op center door and fell forward on his hands and knees. Cross placed his boot on the man's back, pressing him to the floor.

Walker came forward, planning to pull Cross back, but stopped when he saw the commander's rage had vanished. Without saying a word, Cross yanked the mercenary's arm up at an awkward angle and zip-cuffed it to the safety rail. Then he brushed past Walker, picked up the mercenary's MP5 and hurled it off the walkway. It clattered down through the superstructure and ended with a splash in the darkness.

"Move out!" Cross growled. He turned and walked back the way the fireteam had come, not bothering to check on the hostage in the op center or the bound mercenary whimpering at his feet.

Yamashita fell into step behind Cross without a word. Brighton and Walker hesitated a moment and exchanged a look.

"Yikes," Brighton said.

"Let's move," Walker said.

From the sound of it, the Seahawk helicopter was less than a minute out. *That means the Cubans are on their way,* Walker thought.

5514.108

INTEL

DECRYPTING

12345

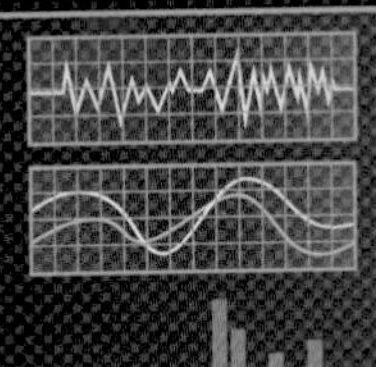

COM CHATTER

- ARMY RANGER – elite soldiers who have graduated from Army Ranger school
- CREED – a saying, or a system of guideliness that an individual or group lives by
- ROGUE – if a soldier goes rogue, he or she acts independently and without the consent of his commanding officers

3245.98

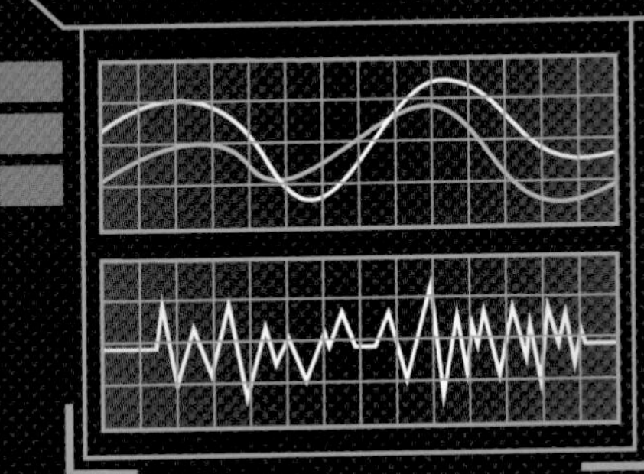

CHAPTER FIVE

1324.014

EVAC

The Seahawk was halfway home. Since the team had left the *Black Anchor,* Cross had sat in silence, staring down at the shrouded, lifeless form resting on the deck below him.

Second Lieutenant Neil Larssen had lived long enough to be brought onto the helicopter, but he'd died only a few minutes out over the water.

Walker had been trying without success to think of something to say to Cross that didn't sound forced. But no matter how hard he tried, he couldn't think of anything.

"We shouldn't have left them," Cross said. He looked up at Walker. "We should have brought all those Hardwall thugs back home with us to answer for what they did."

"That wasn't the mission," Walker said. "We had to do it this way so the Cubans could take credit for the rescue. Letting them save face is supposed to offset the damage Van Sant's people would've done to our country's reputation."

"But if we'd brought at least one back," Cross argued, "we could've had him give evidence against Van Sant and bring the whole organization down. But now all Van Sant has to do is claim they went rogue and condemn their actions. He'll probably get away with everything."

"He might try that," Walker admitted. "But even if he pulls it off, I think Hardwall Security is about to find itself on some government lists. You know, the kind that make it very hard to find good work."

"Maybe," Cross said. He sighed. "What a mess. This whole thing is going to be a diplomatic nightmare."

"Let the State Department worry about that," Walker said. "Just remember that for your part, you did everything right."

"Not everything," Cross said quietly. His eyes went back to the body at his feet.

"That wasn't your fault," Walker said.

"'*The lives of my teammates and the success of our mission depend on me,*'" Cross said, quoting from the US Navy SEAL creed.

"'*In the worst of conditions,*'" Walker said, quoting a different section, "'*the legacy of my teammates steadies my resolve and silently guides my every deed.*'"

"'*I will draw on every remaining ounce of strength to protect my teammates,*'" Cross countered. "I didn't protect him, did I?"

"Knowing full well the hazards of my profession, I will always strive to uphold the prestige, honor, and esprit de corps of my regiment," Walker said.

Cross raised an eyebrow, though he didn't lift his gaze. "What's that from?"

"The Ranger creed," Walker explained. "I'm not sure that's exactly how it goes, but that's the general idea behind it. Neil was a Ranger . . . wouldn't you say he lived up to that standard?"

"Always," Cross said.

"Then mourn him, and honor him," Walker said. "But don't make his loss about yourself. If you start down that road, you'll end up feeling guilty whenever you look around and don't see him. Trust me: I've been right where you are now."

Cross was quiet for a long while, apparently considering the chief's words.

Bit by bit, Cross seemed to relax a little. He looked up. "Does that mean we actually have a second thing in common with each other, Chief Walker?" he asked.

"Something else?" Walker asked. "What was the first thing?"

"The fact that we're both SEALs, of course," Cross said.

Walker smirked.

"Well, don't get ahead of yourself, Commander," Walker deadpanned. "I'm an *SDV* SEAL after all . . ."

Cross grinned. "Right, Chief." He took a slow, deep breath. "And thanks."

Walker nodded. "Sir."

LOADING...

2012.101

CLASSIFIED

MISSION DEBRIEFING

OPERATION

PRIMARY OBJECTIVE

- Secure the oil rig platform and transport hostages to safety

SECONDARY OBJECTIVES

- Minimize damage done to Hardwall mercenaries

× Avoid contact with the Cuban and Chinese forces

STATUS

2/3 COMPLETE

3245.98

WALKER, ALONSO

RANK: Chief Petty Officer
BRANCH: Navy SEAL
PSYCH PROFILE: Walker is Shadow Squadron's second-in-command. His combat experience, skepticism, and distrustful nature make him a good counter-balance to Cross's command.

I had to reprimand the other members of Shadow Sqadron for neglecting to file their *Black Anchor* debriefings in a timely manner. But overall, they performed admirably in the field. All the hostages were recovered unharmed, and the men kept their emotions under control even when one of our own was shot down. Cross was really shaken up over losing Larssen. We all were. But we were able to keep it together and complete the mission.

Second Lieutenant Neil Larssen was a good man, and a good soldier. He will be missed.

- Chief Petty Officer Alonso Walker

ERROR

UNAUTHORIZED

USER MUST HAVE LEVEL 12 CLEARANCE OR HIGHER IN ORDER TO GAIN ACCESS TO FURTHER MISSION INFORMATION.

2019.681

CARL BOWEN

Carl Bowen is a father, husband, and writer living in Lawrenceville, Georgia. He was born in Louisiana, lived briefly in England, and was raised in Georgia where he went to school. He has published a handful of novels, short stories, and comics. For Stone Arch Books, he has retold *20,000 Leagues Under the Sea*, *The Strange Case of Dr. Jekyll and Mr. Hyde*, *The Jungle Books*, *Aladdin and the Magic Lamp*, *Julius Caesar*, and *The Murders in the Rue Morgue*. He is the original author of *BMX Breakthrough* as well as the Shadow Squadron series.

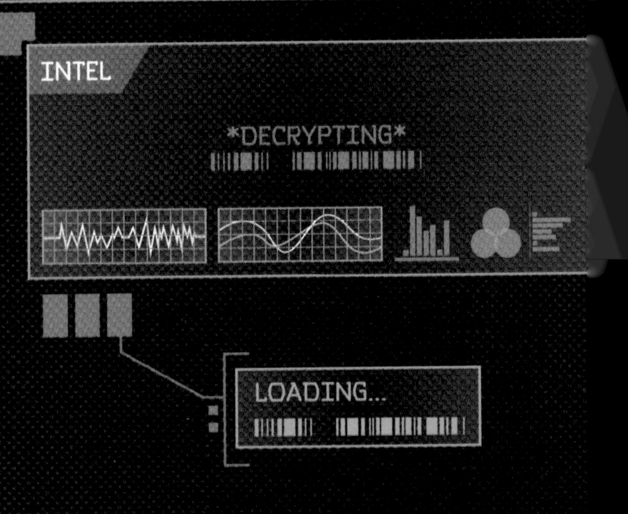